God Endorsed

My Last Writings

by

Stephen L. Lewis

Inspiration Inspires Writing From The Heart

Preface: Though most of the short writings invoke God a lot, this is not a religious book. It is a book for anyone that likes to deep think or have deep thoughts about life and its meaning, yet, it has some interesting and different story lines. Maybe someone can get some new ideas from them and make them longer in nature. I have included many quotes, as well, that are based along the same line: invokes God but is intended to get one to do some deep thinking about life, in general. The writings are short in free prose style of a personal nature. These writings will mostly likely be my last writings, therefore, the sub-title. Mainly, didn't want these writings to be lost forever without anyone having a chance to read them. Even if only one person gets anything from them, it is worth it. I, also, included some of my old writings from years ago for the same reason. Points of interest: the short writings were inspired by a true love and most are about true love, some terms used are from the Old English dictionary, not American English, also, some terms are from the Urban Dictionary site on the internet.

TABLE OF CONTENTS

Table of Contents (continued):

EXTRA: Some Old Writings, from years ago (no listing).

"The hardest thing in life is being true to oneself, for that, we must overcome many fears," - Stephen Lewis

Only One Shot Left:

As the days, years and centuries go by, like most things in life,
God will shrug His shoulders and say, "Only One Shot Left" when a
Will it come a roll of the dice, let's waste not a day a moment a
Wish or dream grab things of God's values true treasures as found
And offered by Him tomorrow may not be another day, on that day a
Satan will rejoice as the gates of Hell will be opened wide plans
Should be not to be in line, when saying only one more chance God
Will pray to he and she, to men, women, children listen never had
God lost let's not there be a first, think not of what to come an
Endless quest should be change to the Will of God was always wish
Of the betterment of mankind to be what he should be close to God.
As the voice on the line finally opened up and spilled guts eating
At him he the listener heard with his ears only half his mind most
Of his heart memories of his run through blasts here, there, front
Back, shells whizzing by shake of his head bringing him to reality

Comfort compassion poured in return to voice on the line crying as
A child war PTSD minutes to hours from the deepest regions of soul
He patiently listened and raised up the understanding tenderness a
Way with words to ease the pains torments over the line took these
Did he into his dungeon of self-infliction it ever-growing yielded
Back to those needing the light the magic of an uplifted spirit of
Inner peace inner acceptance of self and The Lord Master of Spirit
And of Earthly Heaven but his spiritual dungeon chamber of torture
Of self could take no more but it did for he only had self of non-
Caring innermost hatred of life for loneliness will do that with a
Captivation of an Angel he had the voice on the line wiping tears
And showering out "thank you's" and God bless! as he drove home an
Exhausted man he spoke to his only friend may we say sarcastically
For he was no friend as he always ended their talks "Only one shot
left" Satan winked in a flash of bye for even Satan could not stand
The Hell behind his door into house he walked darkness emptiness an
Air of unbelievability no pets nothing of breathing inside into the
Corner of blank room crouched he with feet running to escape blasts

From above running running without stop until tripping
from a gun a
Laying in his path horror never seen before by anyone
took hold of
His face the face of his friend the lucky one for only one
shot was
Left in the gun either him or his friend would escape with
death of
Quickness or be tortured by many means of pains his
friend won with
Paper over rock when caught dragged to friend then face-
to-face saw
Each other but only one had eyes a kick of a door and he
was saved
Or was he and with that he stood up and walked to a
drawer opened a
Gun layed only one shot left as all other chambers have
been tried
As hand started down a knock at the door strangest
struggle mind an
Over hand as he opened the door stood she a rank and
service knew a
He not and with sternest voice "Atten-hut!" snap did he
circling a
Did she "Only one shot left, but not today! I have orders,"
said a
She he saw three stripes of the weirdest kind with a wing
in the V
Something new thought he "Keep 'em eyes straight," she
tapped with
A swagger stick "We're going on a hike," as she kissed
him greatest
Of compassion understanding and love for she was his
guardian Angel
From above and through all fell in love, God told her "He
has only

One shot left, You!" as he awoke from her kiss the white puppy dog
Licked his cheek and child laughed and laughed as Mom whisked them
Away "Let's have dinner, darling," said she with a wink to The Lord.
-- Stephen Lewis

"The magic of Heaven is in the believing of God, for in believing in God, all is possible!" - Stephen Lewis

Treasures - Simple Things in Life:

The Eyes of God sees all things! sees truth, rights and wrongs, all things
In the hearts, minds and souls of men, God is Spirit of which men travel a
Lifetime and only few discover the true spirit of God and even fewer lives
In His spirit before Heaven, the fewest of all who lives with another love
In that world of only which we can imagine, dream and wish to discover and
To discover it we must live it we must become it together the it being our
Love of One as One believing in the simple things of life for knowing this
We receive all treasures of the world, of God, for God is a simple man and
The Key to His world a simple thing, a laugh a smile a spark in an eye and
The hug of a mother and child but more this the spirit all process essence
To God's Key, God's Spirit before Heaven, the meaning to true treasures of
Life few see yet how much simpler can God be, Satan

preys false treasures.

Smoke filled the air above the deck as guns fired and fired
between ships

Of Buccaneers and merchant ship of more than goods
being warship of better

Days Laffite cared not as he directed more shots steering
of his ship and

Soon the smoke cleared and Laffite stood tall at the head
of merchant ship

And brought to him the treasures below lucky day for him
and his men value

Untold where to hide the treasures until the day of
finding again, cough a

Did he of a last as asked where his treasures of that day
one a word heard

"Bayou?" with closing of eyes, browning paper lines of
fainting black word

In French at top 'Map' he held open to see where next
little unclear glass

Of magnifying still not clear guess take place tomorrow
tonight rooms look

Down upon the square as they sat of drinks until time of
sleep talking and

Talking of the find of the treasures and in she walked a
Lady of Mystery a

Woman of knowing of the man of the treasures before the
forces of drinks a

Took them over she highlighted the life of Laffite which
none knew how did

She of so many points of facts or were they accompanying
and assisting him

To the steps did she though weary eyed he took notes in
his heart of her a

Queen he felt in her charms and moves of grace and when
she spoke the word

"Goodnight" there was more he could sense something

above earthly no not a
Night of that but something eternal and more in the morn
breakfast coffee
Awoke them all to a start of hunting again as driving to
spot of map more
Of personal words spoke he and she something there for
sure examining map
Once more he was at a lost so asked she with closing of
eyes trance maybe
Pointing to spot off map puzzled he as X looked on map
there but no she a
Said it is there hesitate did he prodding so slowly as
moving along a mad
Not she another puzzle he why not in time the spot they
got an open field
How lucky as his men ran off to owner find he and she
talked some more an
Opening of selves to each other for whatever reasons
though she minded not
It seemed like knowing or feeling more back came them
signed paper to dig
And they did a feet here add a feet more and more
seeping of water began a
Tiny bit then a thump of wood they hit digging more
more a chest it was an
One of small oh rubies and diamonds it must be for such
treasures to be a
Mystery for sure only a short term more nothing on
outside but little worn
Showing a wood of not known when all examined
photoed time to open it was
With a simple lock of simple thing the chest opened and
all amazed a sight
Of non-belief simple things in life then marbles, tiny
dolls, rings, dice,
And a special one all of wood this can't be! all said except

she all said
There must be more except she away they all took except
he and she as felt
In hands wonders found that special one of what a
wooden chain three rings
Of two end larger rings and written cravings of symbols
markings he knew a
Not did she thought he when looking into her eyes read
she "With Rings Of
Two, We Become One In HIS World" why the smaller
middle ring think he and
Ask her did he let me show thee she said with glee of
knowing as putting a
Finger into an end ring raise hand said she to he and he
did repeat after
Me "I love you with Him join me" after the last me a fire
of a heavenly a
Glow inflamed the middle ring and their hands touched
glow shooting up and
Engulfing flames burning their love into truth a true love
of themselves a
Truth in The Eyes of God in true love of Him for he sent
her to him as she
Knew from Him the treasures of the simple things in life
theirs now a gift.
-- Stephen Lewis

*"A writer is not a writer without inspiration, for without
inspiration, stories are but words." - Stephen Lewis*

Imagination in Paint - The Thinnest of Walls:

Michelangelo's hands of speed and wet brushes colored
the wet plaster of Life
And Adam came alive before the finger of God touched,
God of such strength of

Spirit and form, the showing of ages in His face wisdom
knowledge to create a
Wonder of mankind, wonders animals birds plants
oceans lands heavens of earth
So much more for the ruling and discovery of man,
Michelangelo your technique
Of fresco both buon and secco such mastery how did you
what determination and
Will of spirit where did you find 'em your soul for four
years Sistine Chapel
Torments and challenges pains of no ordinary man
dealing struggling of a Pope
Julius a II to complete his works his way some wins some
losses but continued
Did he the thinnest of walls between two men of the
strongest wills in an end
A creation of imagination in paint appeasing God angered
at first God Blessed.
Ding ding went the trolley car in the early morning
sunrise quiet St. Charles
Lined by homes of largest size charm and beauty grace of
atmosphere riches of
Wealth of money but treasures abound of more and in a
corner room high top of
One home he of sharpest ears hears the ding ding of Ella
Mae the rattling car
Of trolley rambling shaking those within as he struggled
of paint and canvas,
Canvasses lining all walls of the floor of his studio all
incomplete figures
Of a she of his mind heart soul his path to God who
taunts him he believes as
Ponders every move thought he makes with hope to be
renewed not knowing faith
And fate which will take place his brush touches the blue
of tint thinking of

Van Gogh and his Irises and many others of blue but not
Van Gogh does think a
He is he lost and loneliness commonest 'tween back to
paint its stroke coming
Closer he thinks with burst canvas flies to room's other
side no more today a
Memory flashes of Cafe' du Monde mom dad and past
days of relaxing days and of
Course Mardi Gras so off went he but missing Ella Mae
did he and wait needed
He must he in a few minutes Allen a trolley car of indeed
scenes sights of a
Living Oak tree did he see what grandeur of old had she
as sounds of stopping
Allen came and step up did he with couple of steps a
shake of destiny and him
Dropping seating next to she who of so quiet looked away
as he composed looks
To please as the waves in her hair unfurled his sails to
winds of feelings an
Eye full to see her face needed he with his best Boston
voice asked he where
To go for the beignets of fame and that so known of
powdered of what he asked
She turned with a smile of humor powdered coconut and
he said thanks smirking
Inside where to go for this delicacy of which she said
toward end of the line
And a few more steps and you will see Coffee &
Doughnuts and a giggle did he
In his mind could you please show me with a playful coy
sure said she with a
Rattle they smiled stepping off he helped her down and in
a few steps table a
Sat they and ordered an order of two with coffees stories
told in waiting and

In anticipation stopping their hunger pains of grumbling
stomachs two plates
Crisp brown three doughs each plate of two and two
coffees oh the first bites
And better the stories without grumbling noises smooth
lips hazel eyes saw he
As memories of years gone by taste of beignets not quite
the same still good
As can be but something missing thought he as she raised
her plate and blew a
Puff of powdered sugar without coconut he remembered
his mom with a laugh and
A dream as he opened white covered eyes to a Saint for
there his portrait of
Imagination in paint come alive and he saw the thinnest
of walls between them
And thought of how to bring it down, The Hurricane he
knew blew strong winds
Within so off to Pat O'Brien's on Bourbon Street strolled
them as he reached
Her hand so hand-in-hand went they onto the canvas
with Life's paints of God.
-- Stephen Lewis

*"Reading for reading sake, goes against the purposes of
reading: enjoyment, advancement of learning and
knowledge." - Stephen Lewis*

A Joke On Man - The Funny Bone:

Anger not a trait of God, retribution and sense of humor
touches of each
An idiosyncrasy of the Man, Satan laughed and laughed
as Eve slow biting
The Apple her eyes showing the pleasures and delights of
good and wicked

Taste being the good enjoying the devouring and savoring
the wicked evil
She did not care and Adam lacking cognizance obeyed the
words of Eve and
Satan laughed even more another slap in face of God with
each bite which
Adam made as his heart beat with the excitement of new
thrills as eyeing
Eve Satan laughed until crying pointing at God God just
smiled as Adam a
Bumping an elbow a funny bone laugh he did not as God
did from His belly.
Softball a nice game which he enjoyed playing and today
with company team
He was ready to play and pitcher team needed and picked
him what a first
To be limelight of game and as the first pitch flew high
and wide nerves
He said next a lob high and wide the other way arm
feeling tight finally
A lob straight and true over umpire's head and he wanted
out outfield he
Went and worse of all bumping elbow on steering wheel
after game end and
Funny bone slapped him good he heard God laugh, rose
Valentine at door a
High school class his English and his teacher looked his
way as puzzle a
Face he had next day a 'Thank You' card he knew not why
where asked his
Sister was the rose for mother as she missed that day red
face was he on
Report card day a 'B' he knew not how hitting elbow on
desk funny bone a
Real yell of silence in class and he heard God laugh, so
many times life

Of his full of funny bones and hurts and each time he
heard God laugh an
Overly laugh he felt more with each laugh though it ate at
him loved God
More each time did he but tonight another beer after
another beer needed
He to wash down the meat he ate she sat on stool right of
him asked beer
Is what I need and in her voice he heard an Angel sing to
his heart beat
Of rhythm within his being turning to talk his elbow
popped the bar with
Of course his funny bone and jump did he awaiting the
laugh from God but
Instead she laughed soft giggle of glee within an hour a
table went both
And talked and talked with laughs and stares of interest
of each until a
Closing did come down the road to hotel went they
shaking hands in hotel
Lobby next morning met her at breakfast table as sitting
hitting elbow a
Cross the edge funny bone he shook with rub as she
laughed soft giggle of
Glee and God was silent again dazed was he wondering
why the change until
Her voice asked he was thinking what all forgot did he for
a day enjoying
Her at hotel end of day asked for the next day leaving
must she for a day
Maybe the next day in morning rays of lobby stood he I
will drive today a
For you no she said but he insisted easy she gave in for
she loved being
With him off they went where he knew not as directed did
she soon airport

Came in sight there destiny of destination went they at
gate waited them
A child of grandest smile had she "Mommy!" as she
jumped into her arms a
Warmest and tightest of hugs greatest of moments yet
she held back a look
To him not knowing to expect what as leaning elbow on
pole funny bone hit
But jump not he his eyes fixed on her laugh soft giggle of
glee waited he
For God's laugh which he heard, "Haha, I played a joke
on man many years
ago, but not on thee as you can see no joke is both she,"
drove off them
To a life of happiness joy laughter and glee no more funny
bones heehee.
-- Stephen Lewis

*"The greatest romance is when two are always together
in mind, heart, soul and God's Spirit," - Stephen Lewis*

Chocolate Syrup - Made in Heaven:

On the 7th day God rested, on the 8th day God decided to
picnic next Sunday,
Saints, Angels, all of Heaven's staff to take a break on
Sunday 1st picnic a
First of wondering what the weather would be? the first
Saint of God would a
Bring the hamburgers of juiciest and tastiest of kind,
ArchAngel Gabriel cook
Would be for God decided upon outdoor grills of charcoal
and propane Gabriel
Knew both and the best grills and grilling techniques,
marinading definitely
Hamburger chicken preparing hot dogs corn shish

kebobs of vegetables ham pork
Shrimp and more ArchAngel Ariel, Sous-Chef de Cuisine
for Chef Gabriel, such
Organizing needed of foods equipment table chairs music
entertainment what a
Nightmare it would seem Charmeine, Angel of Harmony,
oh what a saint she and
All seemed so well but all felt even God something
missing, condiments which
Ones shall we have mayonnaise mustard ketchup all
namebrands cheese dip and
Salsa for the chips and of course Tabasco for ArchAngel
Michael what a cuss
Of miracles and protection maybe from him and
condiment of a 'must' chocolate
Syrup of richest kind for God loved His ice cream and
milk shakes a homemade
Of vanilla His best swirling melting vanilla and pouring
chocolate syrup His
Moment of peace and joy, I can understand for mine too
1st picnic a success.
A day made in Heaven all so perfect temperature sunlight
and prettiest park
Ever seen softball Frisbee with the dog some snobs on the
tennis courts and
Choo choo of a miniature train of smiling children and
old adults smelling a
Smoke trail behind the small train engine that could and
with shift of winds
The aromas of barbeque and grill pits threw hunger into
the minds of all and
Soon a rush pass live oak trees to tables and picnic
blankets for serving of
The food hamburgers hot dogs corn kebobs of all scents
and kinds some never
Of heard of before grilling of ex-boiled crawfish of the

Cajun sort such joy
And pleasure of everyone and in the middle of it all she runs into the arms
Of her man trying his first grilling day of taste who cares for love taste of
The day how bless they both felt for it was never always so this true love a
Find of a lifetime and with their kiss all forgotten of the prices they paid
For even on this day their love grew more a mystery of God and when tasted a
Burger did she of his her love grew even more for it was pretty good secret
Of his little honey minced onions and touch of Tabasco sauce oh pinch of salt
Of course as they walked to the table of others knowing it couldn't be more
Until the favorite of God was theirs chocolate syrup covered vanilla cones a
Touch God added of a lick here, there of the lovely child carrying the treats
A gift from Him a daughter in the middle of their hug to the table continued
The trio to family and friends eating the melting treats along the way both
Laughed as licking down pass the cone tops eyes saw "Made in Heaven" on sides.
-- Stephen Lewis

"Mermaids may be lore but God can make anything true," - Stephen Lewis

Mermaids Are People, Too:

The brainstorming and imagination of God is unlimited inspired by loneliness

And the fantasy that reality is of His dreams and in His
dreams of reality a
Hope of finding a 'chessmate' so in the animals of land,
sea and air and the
Beings of all kinds, mortal and immortal, God created
with Hope, Dreams, and
Wishes of One growing evolving, becoming His
chessmate in His earthly Spirit
World His domain before the Gates of Heaven, His search
one of near His best
Possibility undone by an Apple and a Snake the immortal
becoming mortal from
The opening of eyes to good and evil easy to relinquish
failure of a project
But not for endless is His time and determination filling
an universe of His
Own so in the name of men women and children God
battles Satan and his evils
Seeking to teach ALL those in the name He battles to
fight by His side, Mate!
Claustrophobia never had he felt before with the many
dives of deep he made,
But there is always a first in most things of life some
pleasant many a not,
This one not as his nerves edged him closer to the edge of
falling apart as
Drops of sweat became a pour 5,000 feet a laugh and a
giggle few strangest a
Fish he saw 10,000 feet laugh a smirk giggles here there
25,000 feet getting
Near his deepest of dives fish fewer and fewer as deeper
and deeper still he
Goes to prove his theory and the working of his
instrument of electronics as
Means to test his machine of a submersible of the newest
design deeper went

It until 35,000 feet with a few hundred more to go but if
all is right maybe
Even more now his nerves a calm sea for completing his
project sweat gone a
Good while back having broken one record of speed one
more record to go but
First to find the rock with his scope and numbers not long
it took proving a
Right was he and his machines which one took the rock of
the strangest kind
And moved aside a hole an opening to descend 35,860
and more 40,000 feet an
Outstanding record for sure lights shown only so far but
far enough to see
Another world from above yet here he had to stop for no
more he could go so
In amazement he looked out for signs to see but he could
not be sure of the
Lights below for surely they were too bright and with
shock he jumped back
With a face in the window of an Angel for sure so was he
in heaven thought
He until he saw the rainbow colored tail of the playful
mermaid so maybe he
Had died till now he heard a feminine voice within which
stirred feelings a
Not of his work and touches of love not known before as
he saw into her eyes
And knew it was her with words he understood
questioned not did he and then
He spoke without lips and she heard he knew and they
talked and talked for a
Longest of time as she told of her world he told of his
which she seemed to
Have known a lot of and in their talks he fell in love and
she knew for she

Felt his feelings as he thought he felt hers and he knew
she loved him too a
Way he knew it was true love now time near its end and
he promised from her
Fears to destroy his works and save her world he went up
with the deepest of
Lost heart as he knew he was lost no more hopes of being
saved and God had a
Lied to him from his prayers the hours it took to go up he
had time of many
Thoughts but he could not forgive God, stepping onto his
ship how down could
He get for such a great accomplishment he could not tell
then to lose all a
Faith of God in losing his love in backing to a seat he
bumped someone from
The supply boat aside his ship to turn and say sorry he
could not as feeling
He had known before struck again he jumped so high
turning seeing her smile
And hearing her say "Hi!" and so quickly yet gently he
squeezed her so tight
And with a longing kiss of such pleasure he thanked God
and wished for for-
Giveness for he felt saved, "Feel loneliness no more," His
quest continues.
-- Stephen Lewis

*"A storybook tale can never end in happiness for when it
ends reality awakes," - Stephen Lewis*

Storybook - Double-H:

The first storybook tale that from Adam and the tale of
the Garden
And if not the biting of the Apple, told in a windy night

campfire
Flames waving with each word and, in that, tale he spoke
of Double-
H, and the child asked what that was and Adam had no
spoken answer
Only a frightening stare of what could have been maybe
one day and
But he could not continue with the stare as a couple tears
rolled
Into his pursing lips and a thought of Eve as the story had
no end
And only the length of the night and its drowsiness got
the child
To sleep, Adam woke in the morning to the shadow of
Eve against the
Boulder and hope of another storybook tale in the future,
Double-H.
The glass flew through the air with the force of a rocket as
it hit
Near his head and glass splintered down into his hair he
screamed a
"Double-H" and her face roared even more "You! Your
damn Double-H a
Can go to hell!" as she hummed another glass against the
closing of
The door as he walked down the darkened street with
only a dimming
Light blocks down he thought how things could get worse
as blue of
Swirling lights flashed from a top of a car driving up
behind him
Stepping out two officers asking for him to stop and after
words a
More words the officers bid him farewell and best of luck
for they
Knew the glass thrower he shouted back and "A Double-

H for you all,"
They laughed his walk to the dimming light continued with a huff of
Breath his mind drifted to another time of his true love, love seat
A charm for watching an evening TV an even greater charm for watch-
Ing the TV watcher as she dozed near a sleep wanting to see the end
He smiled a smile of treasured pleasure for she was his answer for
The Double-H a storybook tale from his father as he sat by her side
She rose with happiest of beaming emotion losing loneliness a hurt
She would pay her soul to be rid of as he kissed her she hugged him
Even tighter than all the strength she could find she knew not how
She only knew she never felt lonely with him for she felt his love
His feelings for her as he brought out her feelings for him and no
Other for she had no feelings without him with him a Double-H from
The tale of his father and as he came out of his fog from the past
The dimming light so near he saw a shadowy figure starting to run
To him and it leaped into his arms and he took her soul which she
Gave willingly for loneliness neither will be from now on, "Mother
Wasn't happy, honey," as he shook his head and tiniest glass fell
Down the side of his head and both laughed knowing she

would come
Around in time walking to the waiting car and the
dimming light a
Quickening flickering of a message in hearts they shared
of true
Love with The Lord in His earthly Heaven and a long life
of never
Ever feeling loneliness again for they had entered the first
of
The Double-H being in one Heaven being in both
Heavens eternity.
-- Stephen Lewis

*"In life, we seldom get a second chance, and, if we do, it
may be hell," - Stephen Lewis*

Is That, Magnifying or Telescopic:

Life is like a puzzle with a missing piece or more, puzzles
of
Jigsaw or pegboard pieces hiding from one's heart mind
or soul
With life's challenge of completing the board, a game
from God
Of search search and more search looking here looking
there an
Overlooking everywhere under rocks to tips of mountains
of the
Highest kind from the lowest abyss of ocean darkness to
coming
Waves above in finding the pieces one comes closer
finding God
And finding ALL pieces ultimate reward a Get Out of Jail
Card?
The jukebox music had the place a jumping on the dance
floor a

Field of shuffling puzzle pieces he thought currently dancing
With someone just not the right one so on to the next he went
Until the end of a long night no luck until next Friday night
After a weekend of work and more work starting Monday, why he
Wondered he couldn't find someone to fill that corner piece of
A puzzle he had inside either too much of this or too much of
That nothing coming close, "Is That, Magnifying or Telescopic"
Scope I should use to make a puzzle piece fit he pondered while a
Not looking inside himself for maybe it was not them but him,
The weeks and months and years to follow the Friday nights an
Endless parade of the same floats of different colors never an
One of the right colors never changing his ways never seeking
To make himself better and still trying to fill a puzzle of a
Corner piece not realizing he had several more pieces to fill
God looked down and thought to Himself that maybe a roll of a
Dice might up the game so he rolled a One and up the game went
For on this Friday night there was a new jukebox in town with
The bestest? of music not heard before and as the slow song a
Played she asked him to dance this new woman in town a

woman
She was as all could tell by Mona Lisa's envy of her smile
a
Wonder of the world as she grabbed him tight and led the
dance
"Is That, Magnifying or Telescopic" scope I should use to
make
You my puzzle piece fit as floating across the dance floor
of
Clouds his mind in another world for she not only his
corner
Piece but all the missing pieces of his puzzle to find God
an
Answer the only answer for him his reward a Get Out of
Jail
Card as she whispered in his ear "You are my Get Out of
Jail
Card, too," and with so they became One of true love and
from
Jail they went together to the Spirit Land of God living
life
As meant to be until Heaven all in the rolling of a One,
God.
-- Stephen Lewis

*"Prayers are of many, being of God is special," - Stephen
Lewis*

A Key, Their Keys - Prayers Never Too Soon:

With words, we may say this but we meant that, I meant
that but
Said this, as you see said same twice but didn't mean
either or
Did I, prayers are not of words but of the heart, heart
being a

More than the beating pumping of the blood heart being
soul and
Mind the essence of all of one being and special is is a
heart,
With all its morality of God's good entering God's Spirit
world
Which one only enters with a chosen key from God for it's
His's
Door to open to those living before they enter the gates of
His
Heaven. prayers of the heart ways of living means of
chitchat a
With God and His Guardian Angels, Saints and all those
of His a
May help men, women and children of the world prayers
of spirit
As well all the prayers and embodiment of the being
being A Key
To be selected by God for He is the Judge of those
entering His
Door before Heaven and true love is when two share the
same key.
The ills of the world too numerous to count the weapons
to fight
Them more even still, of the fighters', defenders', arsenal
of a
Choice greatest weapon that of prayer, as he closed the
doctor's
Door all he left with was prayer for no hope was he given
tears
Held back and stiffing of the spine he did and as the
elevator's
Doors closed he collapsed against the back for he had no
prayer
For he pushed God from his heart years before now how
to ask His

Forgiveness without the hint of selfishness, his son drove home
Without a word said between and when home more so the silence a
Killing in itself for both and family as ice broke melt tears a
Did fall for all especially his son, for knew death now acoming
For sure doubts of before gone now how long does he have an only
God knows and father and mother weep as he leaves for walk along
Levee of the Big Muddy as they weep not a word said of prayer or
God "How could He?" all on their minds and on the levee he saw a
River flow with life and death along its way does he pray now or
Wait until the days of Hospice and he looked up to the majestic
Sunset for the answer which he saw not and walked still did he
In the distance a dark figure approached felt the need to hide a
Did he but did not as the figure got closer wavy flowing hair an
Appearance of glow and glee with a booming smile from ear to ear
How it hurt for his self sadness as she came near in passing she
Fell to the ground and he reached to help lift her he saw tears
Down her cheeks burst into cries and he could but wonder so he
Asked "What's wrong?" sobbing a little still she had six-months

Of living to go without hesitation his prayer went up from heart
To God and he forgot of his Hospice sitting beside her in soft a
Of grass talked talked and more talk did they into the night and
Into the morning rays not once did he talk of his final journey
For his heart was with her and fear he forgot in the comfort she
Needed as it was time hours earlier to say bye now they were and
Names they exchanged she pulled a chain with two keys in a break
Of the chain they both now had one as their eyes meant he felt a
Hope so true and as he dared kiss her bye with the leaving lips
"You can never pray too soon and we will never say bye again," a
Believe he did as they walked separate ways as he gave long look
Until next time a haze drifted around her as she waved he smiled
At the sun with a prayer not of words but a prayer of the heart
And God's spirit for he and her were in His world before heaven.
-- Stephen Lewis

"Simple is always simple, but minds of men can bend the simple," - Stephen Lewis

Wednesday - The Awakening of the Neanderthal Man:

Hump Day they say as if it was only yesterday the term

conceived,
All laugh and joke giggle with glee made it to Hump Day
and smile
Hump Day the day from the lips of God for the camel
created and a
Roaming the deserts for a day or two and God knew it
was time for
A coffee break, coffee what a new idea He thought from
beans tree
Oh, what a grand idea and taste so good Colombian coffee
the best
For sure for He tasted all, time back to work as the
whistle blew
Then came Thursday an ocean here, one there, Friday a
heavy day a
Busy one checking things and then the weekend and
Saturday little
Slow catching breath thinking of things missed, finally
Sunday an
Awaiting over to get a rest with sunshine and rays no
football on
This Sunday maybe next week, don't tell anyone but God
couldn't a
Remember the order of days later on when writing, our
secret, and
Not one of His better days, God says it is time to end
about Him.
The man walked from the cave with a big bone club
dragging behind
What seemed to be a woman crying, well what the
cartoon showed an
Idea of the Neanderthal man we all know and love, loud
voices one
May have but her voice made loud sound so low as she
screamed for
Him to awake time for work not even a fond farewell as

tying his
Tie and rushing for bus from stop to office pickup donut here and
A coffee there all the while in a dream day after day for years a
Challenge for sure why some would ask he did not know at end work
Day not a rush to get home so empty and alone for every night fill
With cards, bowling, and girl friends so she said tonight same as
Before but not home as he fell asleep in sound silence unlike the
Other nights, he walked the fields of flowers mostly roses for he
Loved roses of all kinds he walked miles and miles smelled scents
Of tantalizing aromas suddenly a wall across not to be crossed or
Go over turn back only answer so he turned, a daze of eyes with a
Shock of wilting colors and browns of dried petals a brisk walk an
Up slow drag on down back the dying flowers endless death without
Blood but death the same head down low then a sight of sparkling
White, red, pink and yellow roses surrounding colors of flowers of
All types all alive as him stops of smells and looks of wonders of
Life tired now so laying down in the greenest soften grass laying
His head back and felt did he a lap of gentle cloth and fingers a
Stroking his forehead and looking up he saw his dream of

life and
Living so he must be in heaven not a dream spoke she did
not need
Not for she spoke with her eyes of deep love and he fell to
sleep
With a kiss of her lips awakening of the Neanderthal man
for when
He woke to the alarm of her scream his was louder as he
stood in
Her face "We must talk," as he threw his luggage in the
cab life
Anew scared him not, a faint voice he heard "Where to?"
his heart
Dropped as he threw out a hotel name and after the
shaking of his
Head and falling into seat he sat back feeling the road's
bumps a
Down and up even with the shakes and bumps he saw her
face on taxi
Permit as he dazed "Can't be," with a stop and paying of
fee he a
Gave her sixty keep the change with a business card with
his name
As he looked back into her eyes she put the card in her
shirt top
Pocket and tipped her hat bye and he walked away with a
smile and
Glanced at his watch today Wednesday his lucky day for
he knew he
Was God Blessed and she was sent by Him in answer to
his prayers.
-- Stephen Lewis

*"With the best of intentions, God created man, but Life
seems to have a mind of its own," - Stephen Lewis*

With the Best of Intentions - Tears of a Guinea Pig:

Spring cleaning in Heaven a sight to be seen,
housekeepers and maids,
Custodians and concierges, stewards overseeing all, vast
lands of all
Holdings of God, houses, condos, homes of many kinds,
offices here or
There, one tiny building so unseen far corner of ending
golden roads,
Beginning floating flowing rivers of clouds to amusement
centers and
Fun parks of unimaginable kinds, this tiny building
center of it all,
Unsightly unlike the glorious gleaming high rises of
Saints and Angels
And those of high rank, unlike the simple platinum and
gold of God's
Abode, enter the odd-job man to the building engraved
copper letters
Pronouncing 'Blueprint Vault' to clean silver dust off
cabinets aged
Before creation of Adam and Eve with the best of
intentions did he a
Straightened file atabbed Platypus and discovered did he
an innocent
Overlook of God for name guinea pig ataken already
before Platypus a
Name of last resort a blended mixture of God's
imagination and humor
Platypus of beaver tail, duck beak and web feet so many
oddities God
Lost count God laughs in memory of the volunteer now
named Platypus.
She awoke of the greatest glee first day of work downtown
bus awaits

With red carpet as she does breakfast her majesty if only she was as
She acted and thought she dressed as though she was a queen soon she
Was on the bus to the glamorous hotel's hair parlor loved by all but
Never did hair before did she, stories and words back and forth soon
Friends she had now volunteer needed she with a flick of a wrist and
A swirl of long tinted streaked blond hair he of soft high pitched a
Voice he volunteered as she said yes hearing "Judge does not God for
He has created all," in her heart, did he sit in salon chair smiling
From ear to ear head moving from left to right trying not to show a
Fear sitting hearing a grab of this a grab of that a spray here and
A spray there bowl mix here bowl mix there fear all gone after play-
Ful word here playful word there now stretch cap on sitting waiting
For a master's hair creation 'Mirror, mirror, on the wall," unveil-
Ing it comes chunks of hair this finger and that finger string full
Filling brush as cries echo the walls and tears of a guinea pig try
A laugh between and as she told her story to her man laugh tears of
Glad it wasn't him as he chuckled and thanked God for his true love.
-- Stephen Lewis

"Belief how defined, in words or of hands and mind," -
Stephen Lewis

The Simple Man of Town:

God is such a simple man of the world, His laws rules of
the
Universe a simple plan of a simple man, simple still those
a
Laws and rules of men and women, complexity non-
understanding
Of the world of God not 'cause of intricacy of works 'cause
a
Lacking of the mind of man and his imagination,
knowledge, an
Over belief in his abilities, piety of pride in knowing God,
a
Pride without merit deserving neither praise nor reward,
what
Must man do to earn praise or reward but to find God
and to a
Live God in deeds and ways His simple ways, to
understand God
Is to understand a simple man of simple means to enjoy
simple
Treasures simple wonders simple spirit of His world,
Lord God.
The laws of man are not the laws of God, the young fellow
just
Made eighteen and years of holding back came to a boil
on his
Neck figuratively seriously he had a burn for fifteen years
For whatever reason remember first time conversation of
mother
And father about the simple man of town who arrived one
day a

New owner of a farm outside town and talks and gossips ever a
Since the simple man as of a quiet man, tone of gossips and a
Rumors innocent at first ever growing with tenseness building
To anger then hatred, just the simple things of the unknown a
Not knowing of the simple man this night a beer right after a
Beer and memories of family and friends swirling through his
Mind the hurts and pains but most of all scariness, fright a
Creating of fear for the town though never showing the simple
Man as of a solitary man then next beer soon memories gone of
Replacement by drunkenness of beer and with beer friends there
To be lead and to out of town they left, one and only one felt
The evil to come and though not knowing the simple man of town
Embodied her godly duty for what she envisioned divine off she
Went at a speed the fastest a heart can take off and beat them
She did to the home of the simple man of town and the bell she
Rung around the corner of home did he show with greeting of a
Simple man of town as they spoke both knew there was more than
The threat of beer creation, they talked and talked for hours

And hours until daybreak discovering knowing and
feeling their
Hearts for she a simple woman of town mentioning her
divine of
Feelings she feared but unrightfully so for he too had
such of
Those feelings and when they heard the beer crew
stopped by a
Miracle of empty gas tanks they felt divine and smiled
both of
Them simply then amazed smiles as hugs brought eyes
together a
Closeness never felt before true love sparked by Him, The
Lord.
-- Stephen Lewis

*"The mirror reflects one's soul but our eyes may not see
the truth," - Stephen Lewis*

Mirror Called Ego - World of Angels and Saints:

Once upon an age towards the beginning of time of
creation,
After the ingesting of an Apple the coming good and evil
of
Knowledge of the two, God created special mirror called
Ego
To which to better man and woman to accomplish His
dream, a
Dream for Him solely to know a mirror showing man and
woman
Themselves their inner being to which to see their good
and
Evil to better Thyself sayth The Lord in the night the time
Of most evil Satan metamorphosed into the Snake once
more a

Move not to be seen for altering of mirror to one of circus
Of distorting truth into forms of righteousness and
saintly
To which to judge others fool not did Satan The Lord for
He
Sees all and saw Satan's work beforehand the challenge
need
Of the Angels man, woman to see true self needing not
help-
Ing of God to find one's soul of kindness, truth of The
Lord.
The love of family, women and men the kindness of a true
man
Of The Lord, two weeks of trim eating and fitness of
walking
He lost the pounds of three and new wardrobe of course
need
He and tightest of shirts and pants humdinger of a sight
was
He proudest of self and happiest of could be, circus
mirror
He saw not, those who saw the reflection of him in Mirror
a
Called Ego those who considered oneself Angels and
Saints a
Saw the comic figure of a soul the reflection of thyselves a
Shooting straight-thru for none at all for in their eyes saw
Not a reflection but a mirage of model figures and faces to
Match as they all walked the halls and stares and sounds
of
Snickers tee-hees for the Mirror Called Ego reflected not
a
Toilet tissues trailing down hall behind their short legs a
With long unshaved stubs or beer-bellies overflowing a
belt
Hanging almost to knees, Mirror Called Ego shows not

truth
But image of self and God laughed at the true self of those
Who laughed at finest of God's man, a man with a love of
a
Woman who saw his image in the Mirror Called Ego and
saw a
What only God could see the finest of a man with a
woman of
A finest of woman both a reflection of God's Blessed
Spirit.
-- Stephen Lewis

*"Hump day is every day we wake to the sunrise with
hope to make it to the sunset," - Stephen Lewis*

In the Eyes of God - Merit of Beliefs:

God is not for those who say they believe, God is for all
Of men and women who act and live as in His beliefs,
love
Of life, living of all creatures, in being true to a Self,
The words of God are not spoken except through the
heart,
Nor are they written by man, only in the mind of The
Lord
Forever set in stone, God interprets His laws and rules,
God enforces His laws and rules, and final judgement will
Be based upon His laws and rules, merits of men and
women
The scoring card of the Man, "Good deeds regarded as en-
Titling someone to a future reward from God,"* and what
a
Greater reward than the reward of eternal life in heaven.
Hour in a hot sun walking the side of the road sweat
down
His temple aside brow not the temple of worship he

swore
Never to enter again, heat of his head burning not much a
From rays but the hurt of lost love within, life forever
Known living to faith and in faith losing her why? pray-
Ers unanswered, walk ending near shadowy tree then
watch-
Ing deer running through the field into stalks of corn a
Never to be seen again cooling of his head need for drink
Of cold store few steps ahead while he waits sweat cold a
Bottle root beer to die for and up drove the bikes noise
Ablazing kicking the stands righting the wheels glancing
At man's hat of dress "Not today," says he with a swing a
Hitting the first face then next like a hurricane winds a
Never ending in his mind only as the bikers entered store,
That night curses of God had he forsaking his past words
He lost his faith, there was no God, only that of Satan an
Evil that all exists, more weeks months of words of hate
And claims no God best of friends to all deeds overflow a
List of any man no church but a heart of gold, months
now
Years all the same hurt of lost the door opens he holds a
Side for her uncommon to eyeball anyone he did lost hurt
He lost into the abyss of her absorbing face "Thank you,"
Capped his transformation into a glob of low how do you
a
Ask God forgiveness after so many years with a tip of an
Eye she caught his slump and turned "What's wrong!"
with-
Out a sec thought he opened up to her at table of coffee
And with his name she knew his goodness from all
hearing
She had done "A forgiveness need not ask," words are but
Empty words unless words of God deeds of good from
one's
Heart their essence of being beliefs definition of good
Deeds not wordy words, the brightness of his smile such

A reward for helping him which she could not
understand,
Helping him finding God again she felt years of helpless-
Ness swept away, years of so much hurt but how, not her
For sure how did she, he tempted fate he took her hands
And as they touched, "Merit, in My eyes, you so deserve
Each other, mark scoring card Self by the Man, I score
Both a judgement into the Land of God's Spirit and when
Comes final judgement a Blessing eternal life together."
-- Stephen Lewis

*"Art is anything that brings joy and pleasure to your
eyes, mind and heart," - Stephen Lewis*

Immaculate Unification: Through the Arts -

With written words man attempts the impossible of being
God and creates,
"So they are no longer two, but one flesh, therefore what
God has joined
Together, let man not put asunder," puts asunder in His
name does man an
Artist paint and sculpture attempts works of perfection
but all fail in
Perfection for god not they, only with God may man find
the consummation
Of his joining together, though immaculate unification
through God only.
Travel does he throughout the world's museums of the
finest arts finest
Forms of figures man has created and then through those
of not finest of
Art not finest of forms looking seeking inspiration to his
spirit to aid
It to become alive for he has long been dead in soul, from
The Musée du

Louvre in Paris and the stary stone lonely eyes of Mona
Lisa to a soul
Seeking pair of hungry eyes of van Gogh in a straw hat at
the Met years
Of years travel and walking feet the hatred of air flight,
New Orleans a
Museum of fine arts, NOMA, today a first but before the
first a first of
The French Quarter of old history, Jean Lafitte, a pirate
of charm, and
Old Hickory of Andrew a riding of his steed with pointing
to the artists
Lining the square all around to frontage of Saint Louis
Cathedral as he
Walked against the wrought iron fence he saw his spirit
within reach of
The portrait of such illuminating beauty for the
inspiration he felt in
His heart all pinned behind the walls of solid flames
being brought down
As he stared and stared awaiting the artist to turn
finishing portrait a
Young child of long hair with last brush stroke the
smiling child arose
To hug of the painter, "Mommy, it's so great, I love you!"
what a sight
He had feelings for mother and child moments which
brought tears to his
Eyes for a mother's love he never felt but back to his
inspiration the
Key to opening his spirit to God there in a painting with
fear beginning
Of a new journey to find her first the acquiring of the
colors of face,
Of eyes, of smile, and oh that neck, in the longest of
moments coming to

An end the artist turned and there she was the colors of
acquisition and
His heart dropped to his soul and in her voice he became
alive with hope
As his spirit within began beating its heart again a long-
time coming and
As he handed the dollars to her palm "Thank you, God!"
he heard a reply
Of "Welcome! and more to come," after the last ten she
looked into eyes
"Thank you, God!" she heard a reply of "Welcome! and
more to come," for
They had received a blessing of God's immaculate
unification into world
Of His Land of Spirit the land between earthly-minded
and Heaven of His.
-- Stephen Lewis

*"True love is a true romance in itself, true love being of
spirit," - Stephen Lewis*

With True Love: Travels of Romance -

Eyes closed and all time seemed to have stopped, and
then the colors,
Colors swirling in all shades of light and dark, suddenly
complete a
Blackness of emptiness, open did they to the ways of good
and evil, a
Newness of the unimaginable and the first sin of man and
woman, Lust,
For neither had clothes to cover when seeing the first
daylight after
The temptations of the Snake and with the lust of the
animal within a
Not knowing the evils of it Adam took Eve and Eve lusted

too until an
Understanding of the evil of it all, and God saw too and
knew there a
Must be more for man and woman were meant to be
more than the animals
Of the world and with this goal He created love for the
animals, men,
And women besides a lust to add purpose and meaning,
there must be an
Archway for men, women to enter the Land of God's
Spirit a true love.
The day the hardness of the job how wearing, tiresome on
the body on
The spirit in the body then the journey home of train and
track bumps
Bumps and more bumps with random shakes oh how she
dreamed of getting
Home, with not a word he guided her up stairs to a ready
hot bath of
A soothing olive oil essenced with sweet aromas, floral
notes dress-
Ing down, he rubbed his strong gentle hands along her
aching body with
A press here and a press there oh her mind traveled time
and distance
With pleasures as he traveled with her into the waters of
the tub of
An escape from this world into another and as she longed
for more he
Slipped away back to the kitchen for the next travels as
she soaked a
Way the pains, pangs, and twinges of the day, on the edge
of sleep of
Dreariness he called her down and as she stepped from
that world into
A surprise of woven silk robe around shoulders held by

her man knees
A buckling into his arms he held her so tight a close into a
travel a
Down the steps not a word said first steps a travel into
time a barge
Down the Nile of Cleopatra and Julius Caesar a true love
not of lust
As for Mark Anthony in Caesar she was conquered by his
strengths and
His weaknesses weaknesses not seen by others as he held
her up to the
Next steps she knew his weaknesses and loved him more
for them, in the
Wayward down a warm living room of George and
Martha as the nation did
Celebrate the birth of a new country and Martha held her
man of missed
Years fingers a touching his form though in the spirit of
true love he
Was always in her arms and he loving her faith in him
and Him, steps a
Further down the doves went into an adobe hut from ages
ago in a land
Of unknown for true love alien to time and space as two
inhabitants of
Surrounded mud watched little feet chase the lizard
around up and down
And they laughed a laugh of true love in each other's
arms, all these
True loves experienced and enjoyed as they enlightened
upon the floor in
Front of dining table of candle light and wine and a kiss
taking her a
Million miles away only to return in a flash with the
words, "Mommy, I
Love you," and the child raced to her arms with his

around both for in
True love there is true romance of all kinds what a night
of laughs of
Such joy arising above and into the Land of God's Spirit
as the ladies
Feel asleep on the couch and he looked upon them with
Him as they both
Smiled and knew Heaven in their hearts, He bid a good
night, God Bless.
-- Stephen Lewis

*"The eternal fire will forever burn but may the day come
it is only a smouldering spark," - Stephen Lewis*

Eternal Fire: Burning Hatred Within -

Angels can only hear our words or read our lips, cannot
Talk or know our hearts, souls, minds those are for God
Only, He knows our loves, carings, wants and needs well
As our dislikes, hates, hatreds the evils of our hearts
For these do make God weep He such a hope His
creation,
And as God wept Satan smiled for into your soul there
An evil much exist for him to live and thrive and thrive
Does he in almost all men and women who fight to be
good
Yet evil does win time after time and eternal fires burn.
The first great mystery of the world that of fire next a
Mystery of love and hate, he knew his love understand a
Not her hate much more her hatred of him, her eyes told
Him so as did her words what was he to do as the fire of
Her eyes melted the chains, spikes wrapping his being an
Living Hell and bringing God to his heart a true love of
The Lord and her while a spear she held standing on his
Chest pierced his breastbone a mystery for sure question
God how do you his past sins or previous lifes paying a

Price for if only he knew the unknown would he fight the
Fight for her heart how do you the fight unknown, she a
Knew how she felt but dare she not give herself for what
Was her worth why would he truly love her was she
worthy
Surely not a mystery she wondered him loving her why? a
Why she knew not only felt her past not to follow grew a
Did she a victim no more she saw the dark, wanted light,
The light of the Spirit Satan no more was he with Satan
Or The Lord how could she tell his eyes said love a lie
Could be his actions said not so a mystery to find the
Answer, the only fight he had was to outlast Satan and
His ways for evil has but short winds no endurance last-
Ing the rounds of the faithful and faithful was he she
Being the answer to his finding living, she had fought
Satan already and won now to find God to fill her faith
In Him to find the one with the key to open the treasure
Chest holding Her feelings from long ago one seeing the
Real her, God saw the coming of the eternal fire of the
Mystery endings of their stories, He saw truth of her a
Burning hatred within but not so true, He saw the truth
In him of her but not so true, for her He gave faith in
Him to a full and faith in him for being true, for him
He erased the hatred of him she had in his mind, giving
Strength to both he did, her to be his equal in being a
Worthy of finding Him, him to walk with her side by side
Holding hands with their greatest pride between, eternal
fire burns not in God's Land of Spirit gifts of The Lord.
-- Stephen Lewis

*"There are many keys to understanding love and life, the
greatest being the key of prayer," - Stephen Lewis*

Thimblerig: Shell of a Man -

From the creation of Adam and Eve came the first game,

One created by an apple and an underhanded shuffler of
The name of Satan, a snake in all forms, apples placed
Under thimbles in Eve's head shuffled at a speed of a
Dizziness of pleasure new to Eve through the powers of
Satan Adam watched the game and had his choice Eve
had
Hers too and chose did they choose the same we will a
Never know the middle pick was empty God chose right a
Pick of guess Satan revealed not correct choice a left.
The bluish gray of the evening with an oval shaped moon
Of white he saw but only the outer shell for what with-
In he felt not for he was a shell of a man who searched
For something beyond he could hold but it was not meant
To be for he a shell in game of God and Satan with God
Shuffling the thimbles around and being shell he seeked
For more since he was chosen by a roll of dice by Satan
Granted to him by God as the car he drove spun tossed a
Throughout the air and landed with a winning number
and
Waking in hospital room and not the morgue and since of
That time life spun in the thimbles with rest coming as
In the rising of the thimbles by God revealing to Satan
Which thimble the pea shell of a man deceiving Satan He
Would not for He was God and God deceives not
pocketing
The shell of a man never a thought in those moments of
Rest the holding of the thimble high above nights of a
Great sleep but so far between was spinning of thimble
Along the table of life with the spinning banging walls
Of pitted cap pains and torments each bang further hurt
As flying from pit to pit but in many games rules not an
Always clear and Satan tried his underhand but God
knows
All Satan's tricks for He had learned to a watch Satan's
Hands, with games time is of essence in many neither
God

Nor Satan knows time as man and years of years went by
a
Lifetime to some would he always be a shell of a man or
Would the game ever end with that thought the thimble a
Rose for Satan to see and God in His Wisdom and Mercy
a
Grant some words of hope from her to him words not
hope
But in spirit of hope in this second he formed a dream
Of walking away from the game yet the game went on and
On banging on but not quite so hard how could the game
End but one way only in a dream of her being his savior
Back to life and her wanting to be no hope had he might
She be caught in the game he knew he loved her would a
Not want that anything but that and the game kept on to
Be finished when for him never to be only one way out a
Means of only opened to him and Satan would win win
not
Satan for God saw into his heart his love of her a love
Her of him and God would see an end of the game for the
Shell of a man no more would he be into His Spirit both
Took in by His Hands and God smiled he had beaten
Satan
For Satan picked three empty thimbles for the shell of
A man a shell no more but a spirit of two with the Lord.
-- Stephen Lewis

*"The greatest stories written by writers are their
biographies!" - Stephen Lewis*

Cabin of Solitary: One -

The quickest path is a straight line of no detours so
prayers
Are a direct line to God, but quicker still is being One
then

There is no path of distance for the prayer is from God to God
In the name of the One of God, the One can be of two or many a
Ones of infinity God has no limit of numbers, faces, names, or
Hearts and souls, God's memories boundless in Spirit for God is
Spirit, finding God easy as 1-2-3 being with God so much more.
The cabin stood near edge of flat rim of pasture overlooking an
Icy river below but age has done it in good for storage only an
Awful for that, too, as she walked the path to pasture and saw
The aged sight she fell in love for its solitary shelter of hers
From the dreadful memories of past, current reality of never to
Be but of one, herself, and for dreams of the future of a man of
Faith who she knew would never exist who would bring her a gift
Of feelings of herselves, him and God, envisioned a solitary way
To finding peace in her fate and destiny, examination of eyes an
Opening to the true battle ahead for the hybrid cabin it was a
Cabin of logs in front one side backside and other side of planks
Of aged cypress from land of south and in many places none or a
Rotting logs and planks in spots here and there, wheels aturning

In her head for determination to see the job done and by her and
As little help from others as can be, listed of needs thoughts a
Plenty of making it her own spinning in her mind, tomorrow begins
The journey of proving her womanhood of becoming her woman, none
Other's but herself and him if God answers her prayers, if only
She knew, calls emails that night in morning it started hammer a
Crowbar out the old and slowly fill with the new, from sunrise to
Sunset only with trips to town one day after another weakling one
To body built cabin, just touch up and personal add bits here and
There pride a deadly sin except if earned and deserved she felt a
Proud and which he did too from watching from the trees and which
He did too from watching above, day of the 4th the day of complete
The day of independence from her past, present and future all laid
Ahead with celebration as her daughter stepped to porch and door a
Looking at the scenery towards river in stepping through doorway
The mirrored glass of Alice opened to the feelings of herselves, a
Daughter and mother of One, flew open did the back sliding door a
Vision of days past of a forbidden love but forbidden no more and

Feelings of him now she had with freedom then there entrance of no
Sight but of heart, soul for God sent His drink of nectar to each
A bubbling sensation of spirit for being with Him, all One of God.
-- Stephen Lewis

"The greatest respect to give all fallen 'soldiers' is the 'honor' earned by their ultimate sacrifice," - Stephen Lewis

Touching Fingers: Trips to Heaven

Heaven is magical, in that, you can find it in many places so sayth the Lord,
Dreams, spirits, awakening moments of life, sometimes even nightmares one can
Find Heaven for a fleeing of time, in the eyes of another, feelings, emotions
From others even in spells of hate, Heaven can come to all and all can come a
To Heaven, Satan walked the streets and lands of Heaven, flew the skies stars
Of a Heaven's night before that day the seeking of God's glory, the first day
Of deadly sins of Pride and Envy, pride of mirror looking self glorification,
Envy being born from pride thinking of God, in time one deadly sin leads to a
Next deadly sin, even Satan revisits Heaven in his mind of recollections of a
Better times and wonders if it was worth it all then lust of evils returns, a
Grandest of times when Lord God, Himself, walks the golden streets of Heaven.

There she stood in the shining rays of light from the sun
with all its heat a
Glistening sweat from a day's work, as he did his work as
well the sweat pour
Ing in buckets down shirt, through his mind he did his
work through his heart
And soul he could not stop thinking and feeling of her for
she his existence,
His will to live and then finishing the day opening the
door in such hopes he
Wakes to the swirling of a ceiling fan and his heart
dropped from Heaven back
To Earth, another day of emptiness of just another day
until home from work a
Regiment for years, into the kitchen he walked to an
aroma from out of this a
World and arms around the cook kissing her neck, a
candle lit table for two an
Entree for the coming night with hands in hands and
nearing steps he feels his
Great love for her then first step of stairs a roar of
crushing walls of winds
And she is pulled from him into a tornado of unlimited
hunger and she cries an
Uncountable "I love you!"'s into the wind, the alarm goes
off to another start
Of another day as he tries to forget the ending of the
night's dream in daily
Routine while feeling the night's Heaven, the doors slide
open to a stale air,
To little grocery store noises as seeking to fill his list of
nourishment needs
And a beer or two, or more, reaching to a bottle not of
beer his fingers touch
Those fingers of a long healthy but slender nature and he
looked and saw eyes

Which shot him to heaven in feelings and emotions he
never felt before opening
His life to her through the touching of fingers in leaving
the store his years
Of regiment and routine behind to go ahead forever living
in Heaven for in her
He found God, she did, too, in time both will walk streets
of Heaven with Him.
-- Stephen Lewis

*"With birth, life has many paths, it is the forks in the
road that kill you," - Stephen Lewis*

He and She: On too Above the Stage -

Adam wandered among the animals and trees, Eve
opened his eyes to the stage,
On the stage, actors and actresses have come and gone,
few raising above the
Stage and into another a theatre without acting but true
self opened to all
To see where love, peace and happiness abound aplenty
like apples on a tree,
What makes this theatre so special, actors and actresses
walk and talk with
Director financier backer of grand play, God, Golden
Wings statue of reward.
Writer of the play watched the theatre slowly fill with an
hesitant audience
Of young and old for being a new play one of such off the
screen they knew a
Not what to expect but if spectacular need to say they
were there if not say
They were there and how they hated it so, or to stand out
that it wasn't so
Bad, each a reason of their own they might like it, few

more minutes to go a
Wait of eternity, anticipation a tingling in the atmosphere for off-Broadway
Play, no not NYC the other one, curtains open to staring starry-eyed faces a
Ton of deer in headlights, writer star of the play screams out like Brando a
Human yelping to 3rd degree with agony one could feel and think it was from
Themselves, the lines flowed so easily when they were burned into his mind a
Long time before their writing, then a supporting cast member here and there
With lines he heard and heard years ago, the pains and torments they brought
Added power to his lines, end of act and small applause of uncertainty made
Its way to the writer and he felt good but surprised, act two head held high
Looking to the skies weak yet strengthening faith spoken and hearts opened a
Wide near tears many then walked across stage did she grabbing all eyes all
Dreams of being her or wanting her stopping an almost opera voice song out a
Tune so pleasuring but so hurting so real did he feel her love, her want and
Needs they thought with the lowering of the tune he takes her in his arms of
Hopelessness they could tell with her deep kiss hope appeared in their souls
Of empathy for her closing of act two, applause with a few whistles quite an
Impress, act three the audience ahs as he walks away head held down and her
Crying to the skies scenes of her throughout with others

strong here weak a
There fighting with one then fighting with self
melancholy dreams dashed to
No hope of repairs, as he looked from the wing each word
of hers took piece
Of flesh and some blood reliving her torments and fears,
closing of act four
He was so relieved, tears of dread replaced the applause
with claps to begin
Fourth and final act, she sits head in arms wetting the
arms of the chair a
Figure of cloaked from the rain walks to sofa she sat
swings off the cloak a
He stands and with a voice of such tenderness, such
warmth, such trust, such
Feelings of faith and truth he speaks of his struggles of
change and how she
Brought him peace and love of God how she was his
savior from the fires of a
Hell, raising her head with the greatest of smiles he by
her side embrace of
Believability audience felt if but they knew how true and
curtains closed to
Standing ovation but of one hovering over all others
clapping curtains open
To encore and cast all stood she and him watching His
thumb up and he she
Hugged and kissed knowing higher they went above the
stage, God Blessing.
-- Stephen Lewis

*"Before we can love anyone, we must love ourselves,
luckily, we will be loved back," - Stephen Lewis*

"Listen to Your heart, not to the whispers of the 'little' angels from the sideline, there are all kinds of angels," - Stephen Lewis

Angelica: The Forgotten Angel of Angels-

In the Canons of God the hierarchy of Angels begins with Highest Order
Including spiritual beings of Cherubim and Thrones, of course follows
The Middle Order of Dominions, Virtues, and Powers, lesser beings of a
Spirital nature, final Lowest Order has the Archangels and Angels of a
Same name of Angels but lowest order spiritual being messenger a they
Between humanity and God, servants of the Lord protectors and guides a
For man needing heavenly help, supernatural spirit Angels of Angels of
The lowest order but lower still those Angels lesser than other Angels
Some Angels better than others, all same in the eyes of their Father a
Difference in eyes of man, reach up can Angels be better than before.
He never enjoyed the idea of flight if man were to fly than he would a
Have wings but one must feed his family, an angel of all angels slept
In his lap for this trip would be at night way pass her bedtime, grand-
Ma to see by all means needing cheapest flights as well, called rows a
Did they and carry must he his bag and most precious of cargo, boy has

She a grown, "Welcome, aboard, thanks for your pass,"
his eyes caught
The ones of the flight attendant named Mary by badge,
"She is pretty,"
The voice he thought of his daughter's mother so opposite
so pleasant,
With voice her hand stroked the girl's hair and she smiled
seen by him
With a glow in his eyes, if only no push from behind to
seats went two
Her window him middle no aisle, child slept still as plane
rose with a
Bump here a bump there then no wheels chewing bubble
gum did he ears a
Popping did not tonight, tired but no sleep a book he
sought in back a
Seat he found in front an uncommon one at that, "All
About Angels!" he
Read first page was hooked for reflection he saw Angel
doing no rights
Named Angelica, lowest of Angels she became awaiting
name to be called
But dust and webs gathered she, what a story he thought
about his life
Read more must he, Angelica dusted the dust waved away
the webs await
A call for 2nd chance none to come, tears down his cheek
from memories
Of fights and crashes that came fight more would he for
his daughter a
Not of blood was she but of need, him for her and her for
him, she had
No others, mother was not nor would ever be, he read
more with opening
Wider eyes, and a sniff he smelled such a peace a smell
not of nose of

Heart and soul, he looked to aisle and there she was his Mary sitting
By his side, "Hi, not many passengers tonight and I took a break for a
Tonight is my last of flight," naturally he asked, "Quitting?" she saw
The question before he asked, "Yes, I need more of life," and he knew
What she meant, talked the longest did they with the fewest of inter-
Ruptions that could be, in-between back to story did he, poor Angelica
What can she do to be seen by Saint Peter, with another word he read a
Bump bump bump he felt turbulence bump bump bump more than yellow light
And the waking eyes of child with words of Mary heard by all "Buckle a
Your seat belts! and heads between legs," then ran to his side did she
For it would be her last flight sitting by his side raising his head a
Kiss followed, "I love you!" with "I love you!" from him too, hands a
Held did they, words of "Daddy!" from child his heart jumped more bump
Bump bump again and again "We're going down, we're going to crash!" a
Fact from Mary said she as plane fell and fell and just before the say-
Ing of prayers the plane rose to fall no more, Mary left to see while
He would try comforting child looking out the window, words to her went
Unnoticed staring out was she ask did he what she saw an angel heard he

And he looked too angel saw he head turned to he and
winked and he knew
Angelica lowest Angel of Angels no more and as Mary
came to seat with a
Great smile and glee he heard the word, "Miracle," he
knew all would be
Alright only God grants miracles he was a sure there
would be one more.
-- Stephen Lewis

*"Irony is the difficult time many have in finding God,
just look into the palm of your hand?" - Stephen Lewis*

The Sand Pixels: Castle in the Sky -

In the time of genesis a passing thought of imagination
God created the mystical world
Of sprites, fairies, pixies, brownies and more, all of a
world of man but not of a man
Is one, special creatures of God with His granted powers
of agency, some do this some
Do that, some of mischief some of not, some of blue some
of green some of colors not,
Some with wings some must walk, some of mystic powers
some few less, but all of a God
Of wonders man knows not, even some wonders the
Angels know not either and God smiles.
The pleasant cries of the child "Mommy, let's go!" the
urgency of happiness and joy, a
Heart felt for the mom though strength it took for life
throws its curves which no one
Can out, strikes and balls but never a home run has she
hit and retirement on her mind
With the youth far to go, straining smile she forced while
bags she got a child's hand
Too and off they go to go to go, the golden sands of the

child's love for she was born
In the winds of the sands of time in the Spirit of God and
all He stood, window opened
Hair flowing the airs smile and glee in Mother's Eyes
those special eyes she knew not,
The music played but child listened not, her world her
own letting mom in when she felt
For that was her, traffic of course in time yet the beach
drove up with arms wide open
To them both, today a special day for no crowds spots of
plenty for great moments with
Mom, sands hot on feet even with sandals of thickness as
they tenderly strolled near a
Spot "Mom, over there we must go," the child pointed to a
spot near the rocks no one a
Near and mom shrugged why not, off they went a lot
more walk of steps then the spot of
Point and beach blanket of unicorn spread far and wide
basket bag at corners butts at
Other corners laying towards the still rising sun pleasures
of talk watching waves and
Waves and with great surprise a jump of white dolphin
into the sky "Mommy, let's build
A castle to the sky," buckets small to before wave edge
they took and began the task a
New of building a pride show but hour or two a fun child
a castle had only in heart, a
Smile of mom knew no heart only some disappointment
in not sparkling the child's eyes,
Walk back to lay did she and the child looked to sea in
dolphin jumping a thought of a
Pleasing momma had she then fireworks reds, blues,
greens, and definitely yellows, shot
From the castle moat only a foot high rising from the
sands little figures drabby cloth
Coverings dances to the child "Your wish we shall make,"

in ups and downs of buckets a
Hands tapping or fingers molding the grains soon a
marvelous castle form did it take a
More to come the clapping and helping child so jovial in
few more minutes it is done, a
Castle of none other, one of pride and with a song
beginning with, "We are Sand Pixels,
Daughters and sons of pixies and elves but of the sand..."
back into the sands they a
Went with a shout of "One more to go" ? she child
frowned in puzzlement for a sec then
Yelled "Mom, come see!" amazement the mom but asked
not how for she was saved from down
Below and raised up by child no more closer could they
ever have been with greatest hug
Mom would never let go and look to the waters did she
and the white dolphin jumped and
Flipped times three and to side did she see an arm wave
and wave shock and surprise was
She but knew she was needed and jumped into the sea
fighting waves and waves but made a
She to the arms and grab did she the man struggling to
stay alive she swam determined as
Could be for she was uplifted up saving he she felt his
need to shore dragged him did a
She as they layed drained as could be he said cramps had
he as they turned to look at a
Sky they did meet eye to eye and heart to heart and they
knew their wishes would be for
They heard the Sand Pixels shout, "Prayers to God
answered He, God Bless" child smiled.
-- Stephen Lewis

*"Life is a game but what game depends upon the person,
some a puzzle, some a dart game, surely many others,
but the end game is the same?" - Stephen Lewis*

Life: Irony Defined -

In exploring, discovery, inventing and creation, the
unexpected occurs even for God,
Animals of the plains and jungles, fishes of the sea, birds
flying in air, unseen of
The eyes, too, did God create but ruler of them all man he
created in His self image
Of spirit in the hope he would rule with wisdom and
knowledge with all life precious
As the diamonds and gold of the world but with the
opening of man's mind to evils of
Satan and the underworld the irony of life became of
existence and Hell was created.
All heads of children and women lifted towards the
mountain ridges trailing shadows
Of blue caped cavalry soldiers looking down back the
faces of the weary to ground of
Path of not known and upon the non-looking caravan the
cavalry descended with yells
And blazing weapons of fire striking as does scythes do to
wheat bodies of red fell
To the dirt of their graves for snow destined to cover
them for the winter and to be
Eaten by wolves and others in the spring, in the spring
the crying of newborn babies
Could be heard in the nursery of the hospital building and
with the crying doors up
Above opened in the planes and oblong shapes in the
bays began to fall and as they a
Fell their mouths pointed to ground of their breakfast,
their meal of fresh flesh of
Non-resistance innocent life and the babies cried no
more, as he read the words from
The books he felt the spirits of the souls but where did
they go the Indian children

And women, the bombed babies of the English town, of
the other books he read where a
Did the killed and murdered souls go, the precious and
value of life all knew all a
Spoke so loud yet so little care did they take in taking a
life, of what did it mean
Tore at him, sense none of it, legs ran and ran as the
sound behind got nearer and a
Nearer ran and ran with heart apumping as vibrations
grew stronger and stronger ran
More did they and faster still for death rained from the
sky for B-52's knew mercy a
Not as carpet bombing was not for flooring but the laying
down of death underneath a
Endless bombs, in the twilight between light and night an
ominous sight from opened
Back door of office of doctor protector of life a box is
dragged to awaiting vehicle
Of sinister ills it is put drove to unknown levee and tossed
to the rocks and waves
For the crabs, how does he read these articles and why
seek does he an answer to the
Irony of life, end of another day in the library of escape
from life and the answer
He seeks and in the stairs going down does he as well
when tripping a loose shoelace
And bottom platform he stops face down knees fall near
his face and hands slowly and
Softly lift his head, "Are you alright?", without thought,
"How precious life can be
yet be the world's cheapest commodity?", she just
laughed, "Life defines irony as test
Of God of man," in her words he found peace with God
for he understood and looking a
Into her eyes he saw her compassion for her words as she
once was him a seeker she a

Found the answer and they talked as looking into each other's life through eyes of a
Seeker of true love of a love that understood life and God and loved both and became
One did they over time for precious was the other's life to the other they felt cheap
No more they felt as treasures of the world and heaven, God loved them, blessed them.
-- Stephen Lewis

"There is no sin when following the wishes and will of God, if there was, God would get you off," - Stephen Lewis

Mystifying Eyes: Melting of Stone -

The mysteries of the world a mystery of number, unknown to even the Angels,
Only God counts the mysteries of the world for God creates them in His mind
And spirit for reasons of His own, many have experienced God's mysteries in
Ways they never imagined for being mortal in body, in spirit they do learn,
For in entering the Spirit of God, God hides no mystery He explains it all
For it is quite simple, in entering the Spirit of God one enters His Love,
His understanding, part of His soul for their spirit one with His forever.
The sounds of laughter filled the room for all to hear what a jovial fellow
Was he, life of the party with all eyes on him and sadness of it all he felt
Not a moment of it for his heart was stone, his soul the mantel of an empty

Fireplace, but oh, boy, what a smile dreamed of by all the ladies of dining
Hall to be theirs for he made them laugh filled vacant spot in their hearts
And gave them joy in living, all their toils and troubles forgotten in dream
Of romance him their Don Juan, in stone heart no pity had he in mind he knew
True romance could only be found in the Spirit of God his stone soul would a
Never melt to find a true love of true romance so to be damned fill it every
Moment to pleasure of body and his animal desires and he did, all walls can
Be breached in time but in being damned he knew Satan would fill the cracks
To get his eternal soul, in youth endless prayers went unanswered in mind a
Reason he knew not if only he knew, now no prayers no thoughts of God only a
Second here and there of flash in imagine of unformed glow so went forth in
A life of fun and joy no meaning no purpose no nothing nullness smile still
Did he, broken hearts with no names dashed dreams hopes of a future never a
Possible and not one blink or tear in being sad what a stone was he, night
Of last crawfish tail he went home with lone flashing star sweeping sky of
Pitch darkness of eerie glow of no form in the darkness a lonely twinkle of
Blue diamond suddenly shone through the glow unexplained for he thought not
Of it, blinking red taillights saw at end of curve down the road headlights

Revealing distressed lady of the night "No, not tonight,"
he thought of an-
Other conquest, stop still did he though no gentleman
knew no signals of an
Airway possible here and destitute most of time shrugged
shoulders did he,
In the beams of light he shook his head for the warmth
his heart did feel,
As closer he got warmer his heart got, a whisper struck
his heart, "Leave
For she is no good," yet he could not turn fingers held
him straight until
She turned mystifying eyes of glow of no form forming
into feeling of love
A sight never he seen before a form of no other with
mystic powers of God a
Mystery of Him a count of one this feeling flew into his
heart his soul and
Melting of stone never heard of but by God in seeing her
eyes without glow
He knew he saw her before knew not her name but her
voice in its crying for
Him in her embrace walls breached and Satan aweeped,
and he knew his prayer
Was finally answered when she kissed him and he felt his
heart beat, felt a
Tingling in his soul, his face shined when he felt her heart
beat, her soul
A tingling, he knew both were in the Spirit of God and
both would know true
Romance, true love and enter a God's Heaven to be with
Him, blessed by God.
-- Stephen Lewis

*"In finding God, does it matter if it is fate or destiny, as
long as, we have faith," - Stephen Lewis*

Writer's Love (of Words): Leap of Faith -

The greatest of all man's inventions which is taken for
granted
Is the written language which there are many, photos,
paintings
May speak a thousand words are more yet unwritten who
would be
Able to remember, written words unless destroyed last
forever a
Need to read and understand its only need and greatest
gift the
Writer can receive, books number in the millions,
millions more
To go, writers give us words with meaning yet meaning
belongs a
To the readers, but ultimate is reality which there're no
words.
Words were his first love, sentences, paragraphs added
more, and
The day came of books and the pleasure of reading and
reading a
More, but not all for the love of words for the fear of
living a
Being alive and failing, he had always failed and who
doesn't a
Fail in love, library choice of lunch and devoting of books
and
Reliving the words imagining being loved being like all
others,
Not different and failure of the things he did, reality did
bite
And strike his heart spoken words never could he writing
only he
Could do, writing never to be seen, heart pounding in
words feel-

Ing only him, in words he found his love and they would never let
Him go, the fingers of Satan around his throat shouting failure
Into his soul and words he read repeating the sounds of Satan, he
Could not escape even for the reality of a love knowing she would
Never ever talk with him as his throat trapped his heart, trapped
The words of any hope, how common it became, years would come and
Go as did thoughts of love but never the words, life would go on
And on and never a true love, life of emptiness except words and
Books of words until day he heard her voice of unwritten words a
Harp of Angels played and he knew he found true love if only she
Could love him too, turn did he from her for failure he still was
And always would be, a shriek of Geronimo he heard turning back a
Sight of flight he saw falling figure from where he did not know,
In arms she fell as falling back did he only wall stopped from a
Ground from floor, face met face, eyes saw eyes, smiles of joy a
Both, with dazed voice he asked a what and she said it was but a
Thought, a thought of a leap of faith and she knew not anymore,
With a kick of her foot books fell holding her one arm raising a

Book opened he read it, John 4:18 "There is no fear in love, but
Perfect love drives out fear, because fear has to do with punish-
Ment, the one who fears is not made perfect in love," with these
Words he feared no more, punishment of heart gone, as he saw she
Read the words too, he heard her say, "I love you!" and he knew
Perfect love as he felt God answering his pray of taking written
Words away from him superseding them with words of His Spirit of
Perfect love and words from her heart as she kissed him so tight.
-- Stephen Lewis

"Angels are agents of God and through them miracles occur in His name," - Stephen Lewis

Cupid's Unknown Arrow: Coward of Love

Does God know fear? We would all say God does not know fear,
But man was made in the image of God, man knows fear, so God
Knows fear, as well, yet unlike man, God feels no fear knows
Fear is of the unknown, of forthcoming pain, of nightmares a
Never-ending, and the ultimate fear of Death knocking on the
Door, God feels none of these Himself feels these only thru
His Spirit in man, God knows and feels Love and the

ultimate
For man is to feel Love through the Spirit of God, the
Lord.
A handsome Devil they said of him, he fears nothing,
never a
Fear did he know, braveheart into the land of love,
romance,
A life of wining and dining but never Cupid's golden
arrow a
With an uncontrollable desire of love of a lasting-kind,
not
A loving kind was he, even once he sought out Cupid's
arrow
Of lead for its aversion and fleeing desire away from love,
For she he had no eyes, brute strength yes as well as looks
And body of it too, he hid not from his vanity, being vain
a
Pride did he find in it for he his only one, Adonis thought
He was and in so offended the god a friend of Cupid no
gold
Or lead arrow for this, only one made by Zeus would do,
one
For there was only one, The Arrow of Fearfulness of Love,
an
Everlasting fear of love for eternity why only one, with the
Pull of a string the arrow flew straight into his heart and
A feeling never had before struck him and shiver in fear
did
He for place to hide library did he see and run back
shelves
Of unknown titles of unknown topics of this and that
curled
Into a ball shaking with the tip-tap of coming feet around
a
Corner there standing a beauty of smile and surprise
without

A word flew Love in both directions his fear gone as well
as
Hers too, his knowing Love for the first time hers
knowing a
Faithful Love from him, as they walked and talked down
aisle
Hand-in-hand in her free hand swung a plain book of text
of
Words but much more a book of faith, spirit and gateway
to a
Heaven knowing Him, Holy Bible it said and plain face of
Him
Did smile on the cover saying to their spirits "God Bless!"
-- Stephen Lewis

*"The mysteries of God know no laws of science and
natural, neither does true romance or true love," -
Stephen Lewis*

AfterMath: The Wrong Nail -

In the greatest monuments there are secrets forever
unknown,
Some of purpose of design, some of accident of mishaps,
and
Some unknown by the builders, we could say this of life,
of
Death, and of God, in pulling the nail from the barrel,
God
Chose a wrong one named Satan which fell to the ground
land-
Point up and in stepping God felt a deep pain in His
heart,
In His soul, the wound infected and until this day has
never
Healed, everyday wrestle of Satan keeping monument up

of man.
In days of long past, a boy of such toughness, girls
aplenty,
Money earned, money stolen from dad, playboy such he,
once a
Running through fields chased by dad jumping fallen tree
and
Snake nearly got dad but shotgun instead, laugh did the
boy
From memories of 2x4 upside head, boy gathering turned
head
And there she stood, reddish hair long flowing thin as a
rail
Of bones fiery temper match hair saw him turning head
to girl
Friends, she to be his he knew so did she hard to get had
to
Be to hook her fish, a friend's motor scooter in the tree,
and
So much more until the day of "I do!" a family one day,
child
Came and few more, work and work did he after service
of war,
Badness, drunkenness not completely gone, home battles
came
And gone with the years, one of the few grew such a hate
such
A respect but love not sure, then one year fishing here
and
There, shrimping boating what a fun year, hatred versus
love
What should a boy do, in the years the end came from
lungs a
Filled with history of smoke suffered in death he did not
as
His son did in life, now with nail removed the family

could
Be much more, yet the nail held the ceiling up, it all came
Down, family gatherings disappeared for the dad was gone, he
Brought all together for unlike mom he fought not with them,
The son loss not only dad but family never to be but of one,
Himself, feel not sorry for him for sometimes we all lose a
Dream even God lost a dream hoping one day to find it again.
-- Stephen Lewis

"There are many coincidences in life, but is it a coincidence if it is due to the hands of God?" - Stephen Lewis

Water Bugs, Water Bugs, Do Not Fly Off:

The bagging of the prey and the resulting trophy are least part of the hunt,
The excitement of finding the tracks and following scent, the tease of noises
And fright of the brushes, when will the prey pounce, thrill of the death of
Blood being devoured by the prey or bagging the prey bragging of the moments
Of facing one's final eternal end, Satan will take all souls adding to trophy
Rooms of the fallen but the ones of remembrance those he chased and hunted in
The excitement of will he win, the losing he dread the most for God then won.
Climb of steps, slippery when wet, at top now down, into the waters one goes,
Fear is some for will the water be cold, not today, the sun

bears down upon a
Crystal clear water of pool, jump not but dive in today,
water is nice warm a
Refreshing dip, next the child of fun and joy, the pleasure
of the day with a
Youth of imagination, wonderment, seeking things anew,
but dare not touch, an
Age of beware the new or different, splash and swim,
splash and swim, snorkel
And mask, toys abound around the pool, with the highest
of screech and scream
Filled the air, there is a bee, there is a bee, advancing
away from the bee,
The knight charged into the bee but to find a water bug, a
brown water bug of
A carefree swim, wiggle from side to side tiny feet
propellers spinning with
A speed of a PT boat, with his palm of hand the knight
snooped up the lion in
One swoop, the child set upon the prey with eyes only,
fascinated, dazed in a
State of do not touch, so what to do, upside down red
Frisbee a private pool
Of royal water bug, then an amazement of God, the water
bug turned royal green
As of a Christmas ornament, and the sun shone upon it
back as a mark of God of
His fingers guiding the day, growing the child, upon
letting it go from finger
Of knight, wings burst to the side and flaps of up and
down of a hundred per
Sec, hummingbird of tininess, and with two blinks of an
eye, sky did it flew,
Eyes so wide open both child and knight, more water
bugs more water bugs do we
Seek and did find, three one of small two of larger and

loving Frisbee play, a
Green they became, hugging of penguin water toy,
curiosity advancing learning
And knowledge of child, knight tags along, time ends
many things until then we
Would say "Water bugs, water bugs, do not fly off," with
tenderness they did not
And we learned, as the last water bug floated with the
waves the child turned
And smiled for her mother watched the growing of her
child from pool side and
God smiled for he knew the mother's heart grew, as well,
Jesus cried seeing an
Image of His mother watching him, too, mother and child
the holiness of it all.
-- Stephen Lewis

*"Living is full of condiments which adds all tastes and
flavors for Life's toppings," - Stephen Lewis*

Big Cheese: Small Cloud in Big Sky -

The best perspective is when looking from the outside in,
temptations none,
Satan's perspective looking from within man to man's
outer self, abound an
Endless temptations of pleasing what is within, with
temptations come evil,
And with evil comes damnation but for the perspective of
God and His faith
In man and his need for fighting temptations, fighting
evils, and finding a
Path to the land of the Spirit of God, the journey takes
two for in finding
Faith in another each other, God's perspective they will
find faith in Him.

The big sky filled with clouds from horizon to horizon and
in a small patch
Corner floated a small cloud who's perspective of
smallness intensified as
Viewing his larger brothers and sisters, self-importance,
self-faith, nearly
None had he, with a sleep of hours he awoke to the
emptiness of the big sky
Except for him and as he viewed the horizons up and
down he smiled and his
Heart grew and grew for he was a peacock for all to see,
the world looked up
To him and his perspective of self expanded to the limits
of the big sky and
Pride filled the substance of his cloud, but as floating over
the waters of
The seas he saw his reflection and his perspective of
himself included all
But faith in himself for what did he do to be the Big
Cheese, what meaning
Did it all have when alone no one to share feelings,
thoughts, and faith, an
Emptiness, can there be faith when there is only one? and
with this thought
His reflection glowed and his perspective grew for there
by his side another
Cloud but of she and his perspective now included hers,
he had faith in her
And she in him and both the faith of God, and with this
faith God gave them
The ultimate love of each other and Him, gave them
respect of each other so
To fight temptations, evils of on the path to the land of
the Spirit of God.
-- Stephen Lewis

"One's perspective of one's self is important, but only with the perspective of another, can come the bestest of faith," - Stephen Lewis

Destiny, or Haunting of Fate?

Being of the image of Him, is it not then God is embracive of the image of man,
As fate and destiny are of men and women thereforth both are of God as well as,
In creating man was it done so by fate or by destiny, can the ending of mankind
Be changed or is it foretold to be to be, neither for better nor worst, just to
Be, why then does mankind live, as destiny can be changed by man, so to by God.
In the middle of the night high in the crow nests sat two with naked eyes aided
Not of binoculars, fate or destiny of 1,500 by one little key, a David Blair an
Unknown to most of history did he forget, determined were they by fate or by an
Unknown destiny of David Blair, a shaking distinguished actor of eyes of liquor
In theatre's hall given card to usher in a moment's time Presidential box did he
Enter, fate or destiny of one determined by another, John Parker why? unguarded
Was he, derringer rung out in the laughing by him, Abraham Lincoln, laughed no
More, such one as John Parker chosen that night destiny or fate he for drinks a
History of worst, in his readings why ones of such greatness ended their fate or
Was it their destiny, the writer with all to live for could take no more, actor

Of such renown of pleasing films could take no more,
Superman one of television
Could take no more, when would he could take no more,
unknown fate what will it
Be, or destiny to be changed by him or others or both,
which will it be? who is
The one to know? should he be haunted by fate or hopeful
of his destiny of not
Of what he thinks, today he has hope but what is hope to
fate? there is none to
Be, as he hears and sees her he questions does God
govern fate and destiny or is
He on his own, must he change to change destiny or
change yet same fate, dares
He thinks of dreams and hopes and the changing of
destiny or dreams and hopes a
Foretold of nothing but what will be, he dreams and
hopes of her in the name of
God for himself and her but prayers be they change to
one's world or emptiness
To a helpless God, "I am not helpless yet it is to you for
find the faith in Me
Though to change either fate or destiny for they are in My
hands, in her voice
And eyes your destiny changed but fate is in your Spirit of
God and her heart."
-- Stephen Lewis

*"The funny thing about the funny bone is it isn't a bone
as sometimes a life isn't a life," - Stephen Lewis*

Grandson's Dilemma: Women's Wish and Man of Men -

God had a wish since the creation of man but as many
wishes
They do not always come true, God's wish a nightmare

coming
Of free will of man and the devouring of the apple from the
Tree of knowledge of good and evil, with freeing of these a
Man no longer a man of one, woman no longer woman of one, a
World created many men, many women, watch what you wish for.
The door slammed with wicked swing of an arm, curses beneath
A breathe, question of grandfather of what was wrong, a tale
Of betrayal of fiancee shook grandpa's memories, been there
For I was a man of men whom women melted when with, 'em days
I broke many hearts, four betrayals, four divorces of all I
Regret if not they brought me to your grandma, women wish a
Wish for a man but which man, Man of Men are those who love
Their women with no thoughts of betrayal, a man of men into
A Man of Men did I become with grandma's eyes, never a need
I for a woman, never a care for a woman, definitely, no true
Love for a woman until her voice heard I, then a Man became
I for her, with a smile "Let me tell you my stories," hours
Two of non-stop 'til tilted head and snoozes, grandson away
He took, kitchen sat grandma and story he told, grandma did
Smile until question how she forgot grandpa's divorces

took
A chance with him, a love from God knows no
boundaries, but
A love from God needs to be built as well as felt, grandpa
Tripped a many lights until meeting of our eyes then a
only
Of him and I began we builded, many voices chipped at
brick
Wall we had but our love kept together for he became a
Man
Of Men I could trust as we built together we built each
one
Of us too, my faith of him, his faith of me, our faith with
Ourselves, with God was our mortar for our home we
built, a
Home withstanding the test of time and Satan's evils, best
Of friends not us, best of romantic lovers we became
there
Cannot be lasting romance without true love, scratched
did
He his head, none this helped him, a dilemma he still
had.
-- Stephen Lewis

*"All the words of love mean nothing compared to the
feeling of Love through God," -- Stephen Lewis*

Just Can't Do Right, or Is That Can't Do Wrong?

God is the Almighty God with powers of creation and
eradication,
In the days of creation of Angels, Satan sat on the right of
God
Before the Fallen, on the Day of Fallen, Satan stood in
front of
The Lord and spoke of the evils he had gathered into

force of an
Army to battle God's Army of good, with the end of
Satan's words
The left-hand of God spoke, "Lord, swat the fly before
flight or
Forever suffer its bites," and the Lord sayth, "A wrong
maketh a
Right not, Gabriel," and God knew a wrong or right
doesn't exist
When one does their best, God did his best in Satan but
He lost.
Dad told his son to retrieve the crescent wrench whereby
pair of
Pliers he got, what words of wrong did he tell his son who
knew
Not tools of his dad, these words cut through flesh and
blood to
The heart of the son, son not yet man to understand he
did his a
Best, in time another day, dad spoke for a jig saw which
his son
Brought him a jig saw and not a word of thanks spoken or
of doing
Good, walk away his son head hanging down, he learned,
swinging a
Hand did his mom to a drunken dad, he knew the wrong
spoke up did
Not he walked away, he learned, the dad sulked his head
down with
Memories of past of war, badness done in youth or just a
troubled
Mind, yet son just walked on by while knowing the wrong
for even
Not his dad would he do right, he learned, in years
coming earned
Did he diplomas, degrees and those were right, yet in

heart path
Not taken question was that not a wrong? he learned, words heard
He did he knew his right but their wrong or was their right his a
Wrong, in her eyes he saw only right, no wrong, a life absolute a
Finding he made against all his learnings but yet felt wrong what
His answer, and the words came from the one that knew the answer,
"There is no always doing right or always doing wrong when wonder-
Ing which you have done, exist no rights nor wrongs just choice a
Decision we all make, when finding your answer your absolute of a
Only right you have found God, He is the only Right," sayth Lord,
"In her you found me, your answer to your question of life, find-
Ing me so did she, she your substance as she has My Eternal Love."
-- Stephen Lewis

"Without free will there is no Devil, but with free will is there a God?" - Stephen Lewis

Little Smokey: Three plus One -

World like collected cedar bark for fire, ready to tinder a blaze,
Goose stepping into the Rhinelands to cheers of crowds, 1936 years
Before rise of German power, years after the coming of Death, 1937

Start of the sail to Pearl Harbor and World War II a war
of China
And Japan and more coming of Death and tears of God
for further a
Went His greatest creation from His dream, His sorrow
man a reads
But yet not reads, what God seeks free will of man abides
a Devil.
The year 1936 or was it 37, the blowing winds of the
world touched
Not the little country land of southeast Louisiana, fields
straw-
Berry, corn and more, waterways flowing here and there
fish flying
Out of the water into the frying pan, churches saving
souls and a
Bar for everyone pew, between the cypress house and
barn but far a
From outhouse path three teenish uncles, nephew made
four, match a
Lit cigarette then to nephew giggling glee of 4, 5 year old
choke
One or two then puff, puff, puff, oh, what a face of red
sickness,
"Allen" called out for lunch, soon "Jimmy, Pershing, and
Louis!" a
Yell out for punishment bellowing out of raising
Grandma, Mom, she
Mellow of all so stern, memory of last stunt still in mind
powder
Of gun in chicken feed making bombs, sounds of
adventure of war of
Excitement small boys, small tap of broom straw on butt
of child a
Out of door "Little Smokey, get," from the door he
stepped into an

Oven of frozen hell, bees not, bullets whizzed by amore
deadliness
Sting, cold winter mountains of Korea make not for good
graves of
The many friends he saw killed, with a bursting sound
shrapnel rip-
Ped his leg, "Uncle Jimmy" slapped away the next round,
"Pershing
His Marine Uncle" he crawled to safety, "Uncle Louis"
kept his cool
His nerves, by way of three uncles plus one he survived
the battle,
The war for love of wife and child, when embracing his
wife with a
Crying child he felt the broom straw tap on butt, "Little
Smokey,
Get," prayers of a mother grandma answered, her child
safe from a
Horror of man, war, in his dreams her great-grandson
sends love of
Appreciation and family to her, God for he feels a broom
straw tap.
-- Stephen Lewis

*"The greatest families consist of many families within
the one, right and truth holding the one and its many
together," - Stephen Lewis*

The Child: Sin No More -

Divide law written by the hand of God, governed and
enforced by God, Himself,
And on Judgement Day, God will be the judge
overlooking the trials of all men
And women and their children, too, prosecutor and jury
God will all be, so of

Man, women, children who will their defender be but
God, Himself, and defense
He will use, the gift of free will from Him to them, the
disobeying and abuse
Of God's will and law called sin yet a judgement call of
free will versus sin
What a defense there will be and the waiting of verdict of
innocent or guilt.
The child walked to the gate with escort of state and cries
within not again,
Doorbell rang as a wait followed by slowly opening door,
hag maybe not, close
Could be argued, what a stale smell as he heard the words
of so many times, a
Ritual it had become, room of bunk beds really rowdy
kids but winning words a
Mixture of toughness, meanness, and cool, before the
sleep of night eyes rose
To the heavens with prayer of which only he knew, in
coming days plans drew a
Map in his head, in the early morns open window, out
and down the road he took
Without looking back, smile, laughs, tap of heels, and the
witches house came
Down, blue lights flashing 'round and 'round, take off not
him, ain't first a
Not last he knew, flashlight and darkened badge he saw,
then her eyes, smile,
And a flash of glow in his heart bewildered him, small
town children not walk
At night, ride in her car did he, everything closed except
station of police,
Of one police, her, long talk of pleasure for the ease of his
long story his
Life since parent's death, her voice, charm, connection
unlocked his heart to

Her, longings of her innocent eyes brought memories of his mother he never no
Never thought before, cafe coffee shop opened next door aroma blew in as did
He, the other police, tense words hid not their love but barriers shown too,
First words to child and child saw flash of glow in his heart not bewildered
This 'a time, just smiled fingers crossed, with the passing of the baton her
Arms called for a hug he gladly gave with his mother's forgotten memories, a
New memory he hoped for, her last glance in leaving to her replacement, maybe
Partner the better word he hoped for with a remembered memory of his dad, not
Today maybe tomorrow, "Glad to meet you, sir, she talked about you all night
And I wondered if you were as great as she said," a lie he told, liar, gamble
Took he did, will they work doubt until flash of glow and words, "Sin no more,
Or at least not too bad," a wink from God he felt as he saw visions of a new
Mom and Dad hugging him immensely, showering him with kisses and God's love of
Them all for he knew there was no sin when listening, following God's wishes.
-- Stephen Lewis

"Philosophy is God's way to explain man," - Stephen Lewis

Turkey: The Hunter and The Prey?

Survival, the greatest instinct of man and beasts of the

world,
There are the hunters, then there are the preys, knowing of the
Two which one is is the issue can be the challenge, and knowing
May not be easy; hunters be the preys, preys can be the hunters
And both can be both, Satan distinguishes not, all same to God?
Midday and he looked up and saw darkness, the sky filled leaves
And branches of trees, no blueness to see, adventure he sought,
Adventure he got, loss from the pack of hunters, prey of jungle
He felt at the moment, rations not, few shells of arms, knife a
Sharpened never used, sweat of fear within his heart and mind a
Feeling he felt more with the roars of the coming night, North,
South, East or West, he knew none, sun was none, search of out
Of the jungle began with the search for prey, small hearings of
Sounds heard by his ears, some his stomach others of scurrying
For shelter from the night, strangest thing hunger disappeared
At thoughts of survival for the night, the hunter had become a
Prey, remembrance of fire and light brought not knowledge make
Either, fallen tree with brother boulder made one's back firm,
Not most comfortable bed, in time, comfort forgotten for

sleep
He needed, so much better a warm bath, endless food, night out
On town the bestest friends, she stood with roaming eyes search
For what he knew not, by chance eyes met, continue did his, her
Scoped his form and she moved with a grace and smile glided to
Him with hand gesture to dance floor, another hand gesture band
Went slow, innocent embrace until kiss on neck, quietly moved a
Back did he, "My lady you ain't," scolded her face watching him
Leave back to seat, face metamorphosis to horns fiery red grin
Of extreme anger, wallet photo he pulled "I love you, honey," a
Twitch or itch he scratched waking to light ray piercing trees,
Up he sat face in hands worried whole day of jungle retreat he
Be, tap on shoulder a jump he did, "Where have you been?", over
The hill they were, "Why didn't you yell, turkey?" man laughed,
What a fool he felt, joke they did walking away, "Turkey," he
Heard in his ears as God told Satan, "He's taken by a real love
Created by My hands and what I create cannot be broken by you."
-- Stephen Lewis

Curiosity: What If No God?

Added to the Witches Brew a hint of H, touch of C, tons of
Fe, Au for wealth,
And, of course, a little tip of rat tail and pinch bat wings,
swirl and stir,
Swirl and stir, hours upon hours, decades upon decades,
eons too, then a tilt
Of the iron cauldron the crafty concoction of a recipe
pours into the mold of
The Earthly universe, arbitrary science of this and that,
sprinkles a salt and
Pepper here and there, galaxies and solar systems dot
through with cooking of
It all, in a matter of time bound to produce man and all
the animals of world
Seen and unseen, how could there be a God? Sounding
bellow laugh God had, too.
He strolled hand-in-hand with the lady of his love into
the sunset of reddish
Glow, one word led to this and that jokingly and his love
sashayed ahead, Hmm,
His thoughts went with her if you know what I mean, out
of the Blue he was an
Object of vision from days gone by, he saw himself in the
past as he traveled
Ahead his path was changed for 'what if no God', he
glanced at lights coming
Through his car's side window and then a bang and flight
he took to the night
Air instead of godly fingers gently lowering him he
dropped like a rock and a

Certain death, with a shake of a head another vision
entered his mind, voice
cried we can be no more yet he reached over the phone
and begged, stole back
His love of then only to lose her for 'what if no God', his
life shambles and
Being lost he was lead astray to the arms of Satan and a
world of drink, drugs
And the worst of women, the days and nights of chances
of death being crazy as
Can be with no fear leaps from tall buildings, thoughts of
this and that all a
Nightmare to end his life none succeeded for the strength
of God was his will
And he could not fail God, but 'what if no God' the jump,
slit or shot surely
Would have ended it all eventually, what if he had not
followed God, his life
Definitely would not be the happiness and peace he found
with his lady, savior
Of his soul, giver of laughs and joys, his key to the
kingdom of heaven and an
Eternal life worth living, 'what if no God' why even think
it he thought as he
Watched his lady approach, Hmm, his thoughts came
with her this time as if you
Know what I mean, she kissed him for she knew what was
on his mind, and hers,
With the tightest of hugs she felt his tears on her cheeks
and she thought a
Thought of 'I know there is a God' for once I dared think
'there was not' but
He brought God back to me and feelings I never felt
before for him and God, a
Curiosity of 'what if no God' never crossed their minds
when together for God

Brought them together and connected their souls with a
love for all eternity.
-- Stephen Lewis

*"With faith in God comes just rewards on Earth and in
Heaven, we may not see them, understand them, but in
our spirits we receive them," - Stephen Lewis*

Temptations: Black Gold -

Satan has many weapons of tools, tricks, and deceit, as
effective as,
Can be, yet, his most effective, efficient are weaknesses of
men and
Women, jealousy of rivals and others, envy of the better
off, greed a
Definite one, for possessions such as wealth, power, food,
and people
Through unlawfulness, only through God can men and
women overcome the
Weaknesses used by Satan, faith in God and themselves
defeat all evil.
As he drove his car back to the city for travel home, he
smiled twice,
One for the smooth talking before his leaving and one for
what was to
Become in the future, in region of land without resources
long known,
A man explored a cave for food, with thought of gold a
move of strike
Of pick black thick oozing flowed down dusty wall, knew
not his find,
But curiosity better of him, Black Gold, unbelievable
wealth a dream
Of men, soon buyers and sellers preyed upon his home,
one of a fancy

Car and smooth talking found his choice, talks, deals, contracts, all
Soon done, waving back to lowly man and his wife the driver smiled a
First smile, wife seemed somewhat bright, man not quite so, he shall
Be the one chosen, second smile for the trip to come and future deals
Of only wishful thinking coming through, man of gold exited the plane
To be greeted by the smiling man, to the hotel room all a glitter and
Talk sure of his prey, hard liquor, fast women, unsigned contracts of
Such legal wrangling, golden man overwhelmed then shock in opening of
Room door, loud music, scant clothed women, clicking glasses of ice a
Sign of free flowing drinking, hazes of smoke of the funny kind, "Let
This be the beginning of a great business friendship," as he drove a
Lusting lady to the shock looking man laughter rang out with chuckle
As man strolled to his room, leering women, offered drinks and drugs,
Temptations of many kinds, slowed not stopped he continued his room,
He smiled whole way, closing of doors with another laugh, check bags
Shower before sleep, before empty bed, but not, naked ladies covered
His bed, chasing out he laughed, knock on door he opened, "Man, what
Do I have to do to make you happy?" The man saw Satan's smile and he

Laughed, again, "My temptations are only for my lady!",
puzzlement a
Seldom face on Satan, "But she is not here," this time
deep chuckle
Infuriating Satan's face, "My lady is always with me!" and
Satan saw
The face of God in place of the man's and Satan knew his
Black Gold
Of Temptations worthless to a Golden Love of two for the
Lord, God.
-- Stephen Lewis

*"The tip of Cupid's arrow is filled with Love provided by
God," - Stephen Lewis*

Marble and Floor: Finding Aphrodite -

The arts are found in all forms of life, nature, and the
world of God,
From these arts come all beauties, beasts, and creatures
of the night
And day, from this can come love, passion, devotion,
hate, disgust, a
World of emotions, now and then, with conveyance of a
God's substance.
The best ideas came to him sometimes in the most
refreshing moments, a
Shower for example, walls of marble, then other
moments of stress and
Escape from the world, that private room for the personal
hygienes and
Reading, the floor with straight lines, world of curves,
swirls, and a
Touch of this and that here and there, with the wipe of
water from his
Eyes his epiphany appeared as in sight of the wall in

front, Rembrandt,
van Gogh, Gauguin, Leonardo, Michelangelo, Monet and
even Andy, all on
One wall, remembrances of years of art and the beauty of
it all, into
Another world of lines, curves, angles, colors, media, oh
memories he
Missed returning to his heart, just step back into his
artistic senses
Of long lost, all for another day, need of all God's
creatures cometh,
A book tagged along by his side, magazines lined the
wooden rack for a
Substitution need, with a slip of the book his eyes caught
glimpses of
Characters from the walls of his library, Long John Silver
with wooden
Leg, Peter Pan and his pan flute, the one of Captain Ahab
strapped to
The back of Moby Dick, the stories he saw, back into life
he went with
Smile for the return of old stories to his mind, but the life
of real
Is much more dark with turmoils sometimes, strings were
tight pulling
Here, tugging there, the strings running through fingers
and toes and
The whole of his human form, loves, wants and needs,
from this one or
That one, money and bills, all strings spinning and
tangling around a
Neck choking with living life, marble, the marble, and the
floor, his
Dash to find the one to save him, books, a magazine rack
tossed aside
And roaming eyes found so many characters and stories

yet not what he
Sought, streaming hot waters ran down his back as eyes
and fingers he
Scanned the dripping marble, Eureka! of Archimedes,
found did he that
He searched, Aphrodite, feeling as Pygmalion, prayed to
her he did as
Asking God to make it real, hearing his calls Aphrodite
gave him his
Wish not knowing the true meaning of it, in a blink of
God's eye she
Felt breathe in her heart and stood in front of him,
meeting of eyes
Told it all, God granted his prayer as He did Aphrodite's,
he an one
For saving him, she for one to bring her alive, both being
with God.
-- Stephen Lewis

*"Life is a game and to win the whole damn thing means
becoming with God?" - Stephen Lewis*

Just Reward, Staying the Course:

In following the road of life sometimes we need a
headlight for the darkness,
Othertimes, the blazing lights ahead blind us as we sway
and whirl ahead, and
We can only keep our strong faith God is leading us for as
faith gets weaker,
Bumps and rough terrain can help Satan grab the wheel
and crash our vehicles
Of life, we can recover the road or repair vessels with help
of our love ones.
The app said this way, the map said that way, the sign
ahead said another way,

His feelings said yet another, the rain came down in old
tin buckets but there
Was no stopping, the up and down and the up and down
shot his guts to right to
Left and big pot holes wrenched his heart into his mouth,
he had his shipment
To deliver, his journey to make, there was no stopping
him, but only so long a
Person can drive without rest, along side the road lights
blinked off and on,
Off and on, "Motel For The Weary", sign screamed in
bright red, air hissing, a
Squealing of tires, loudness of engine braking, perfect
stop on side of motel,
Bottom floor room he sought and got, side of pool in heat
of summer, 'stopping
Rain clearing night, quick hot meal then hot shot waters
time for bed and rest
Much needed, dreams of a lady warrior, his lady warrior
flying down to save a
Day, save him from destruction, save his soul, vivid of
colors and so real as
She kissed him before sailing to home his heart skipped a
beat as part of him
Went with her, his heart, she had not yet reached the
clouds when a large bang
Rang out, his heart flopped in his chest as thinking he lost
her as waking up,
Ears aringing from continuous bangs and clatters of tin
accompanied by shouts
And cheers of drunken rowdiness, from open door tribe
of naked women danced a
Round the pool opened doors across, dazed from
sleepiness but not hazed a bit,
Eyes staring upon a man all others behind their doors
with peeking curtains of

Juvenile men, surrounding the one wagon they pounced
upon him, images of lady
Warrior, images of her beauty, of their true love, a trident
of love of her,
Him, and God, gave him the strength to fling hot
tempting taut bodies into
The cold waters of the pool, not a moment thought other
than of his lady, of
Her love for him, his love for her, the unbreakable bond
formed by God, with
The last toss of temptation from the bowels of Hell, Satan
frowned, God just
Laughed for he knew the man's faith for He, the Lord,
had the same faith in
The man since the man's youth, looking to the skies he
saw his lady warrior
Reach the clouds and smile back to him her eyes filling
him with such love,
Such caring, such need, a great hurt of wonderment felt
so good for soon he
Would be home after his delivery of toys, well-wishes,
goodwill to St. Nick
For the children and people of the world, returning to his
door a good night
Rest did he get, hot water of shower, hot breakfast of
pancakes, rise ready
To leave, young lady approached, "Thanks, mister for last
night, apologize I
Do, you made me think some, again, thanks!", just
reward staying the course,
Changing a life to good, he hoped, looking to heaven a
just reward of a lady
Warrior's smile, staying the course most his life he found
God's just reward.
-- Stephen Lewis

"When shopping, sometimes you may have to go with the feelings of God, for maybe, he knows what's best for you," - Stephen Lewis

Logic: There Is A God!

As uncertainty grows, so does lack of conviction, aspirations flounder on,
Morals lessen closer to wrong, beliefs in one's life weakens to a point of
A question, "Does God exist?", faith gets closer to an unknown word, mind
Overtakes the heart, soul, spirit, reality of God becomes reality of real.
Looking into the palm of his hand, reason of it all he wondered, validity
Of the palm, proof, inference there is a God, where is the logic of Him, a
A Lord, a creator, the books, the books where answers can be found, to his
Library he went, four walls of books from all theses, genres, categories,
A world of words, an universe of the mind, in the middle of it all he sat
His chair of comfort, of thought, place of his center of transcending and
Contemplating with mediation to planes and dimensions outwith the body, a
Body of limitations, of weaknesses, insufficient for the non-physical, nor
Touch of God's all, if there is a God? nor touch of the logical, eyed did
He the walls one at a time from top to bottom, twenty feet each, number of
Books unknown but each with a power of their own, the power of books, mind

And that called thought, thoughts with power of imagination of reality, of
Existence, he closed his eyes, these imaginable thoughts began a journey,
A trip through time and knowledge, he saw, he felt, he experienced the Laws
Of Sciences, those of Math, and Physics, those Laws we do not yet know, and
With these laws came the principles of hundreds, maybe thousands, count he
Did not, the principles of phenomena of specifics, clarity and explanations
With theories, theorems and rules, unlimited in nature, universal, formulas
Of numbers, signs, concepts, angles, on and on, before the last wink of his
Eyes for the night, he saw the last law, Law of Logic, reasoning of qualify
of well-grounded principles acceptable and based upon other laws of nature,
Physics, of being, with the last wink, his eyes closed with his findings of
An answer with a question, "Who created these Laws? Who created logic?", a
Feeling which is a thought of spirit gave him a peaceful sleep with dreams
Of lost enjoyment, lost love, lost affection being found and relived, felt
Did he which he questioned, feelings of true love of his lady and God, for
Without his lady, he would have not asked the question which has saved him
In the eyes of God, the beam of light and life came through the skylight,
Arms wrapped around his neck as she sat in his lap and kissed him awake, a

Hug of his arms around her gave her a feeling of love she
had not felt be-
Fore, true love, her kiss went deeper into lips with a
hunger for more, a
Moment between kisses he gently shouted, "He created
Laws that govern the
Universe," sigh choke as she kissed him again, she heard,
but she already
Knew, as she caught her breathe, he shouted louder,
"There is a God!", an
Eye opened wide to see her reaction, the next kiss came
with such a power-
Ful force, again, she already knew, for she and God were
waiting for him.
-- Stephen Lewis

*"To deny the mystical world is to deny a world of God
for God is many worlds," - Stephen Lewis*

With A Thought: Anatomy>Physiology of New Worlds -

God was but one with truest of loneliness, "Let Us make
man in Our image,
According to Our likeness; and let them rule over the fish
of the sea and
Over the birds of the sky and over the cattle and over all
the earth, and
Over every creeping thing that creeps on the earth," and
with a thought,
With a touch of a finger to water and dirt He begotten
man and woman, two
With meaning and purpose, too two of three worlds to
share in life, third
To share with God in Paradise and His gift of free will to
be with Him, a
One world of foundation, structure of form, fingers,

hands, hearts, lungs,
And more, with mind of thought a station of junction to two worlds, next
Stop one of living foundation, living structure of functions, activities,
Both phenomena of physical, chemical nature to the organic organism steps
To World One's junction station with a ticket of the two to World Three's
Destination of the ultimate, but station junction has no tickets to sell,
Price of ticket set by God? the surgeon slid the knife along the chest to
Fix the heart of World One & Two, skin, blood all so normal, in a cut for
Getting near to his goal, an invisible feeling he saw in his eyes, nurses
Saw not, shake of a head continued on, all went fine results for waiting
Lady, she of many years oh so much a lady, tears flowed down her eyes as
The doctor told her good news, as before, an invisible feeling shot into
Her chest, one nearby nor lady herself acknowledged the sight, he knew a
What he saw, as he knew he saw and stared upon the cross on her neck, as
A feeling he saw a feeling come into his heart and for the first time he
Felt God's love, he asked the Lady of her cross, the back she handed him
To his face, "You're my ticket to God's Spirit World, your Truest Love!",
More praises and thanks she said as he felt the meaning of the words, in
The quickest of dashes to his office and privacy of his

phone, pushes of
Screen never done so fast before, "Honey, I love you, will
be home for a
Most wonderful of Christmases...", as she said goodbye to
unexpected call
And greatest of all Christmas gifts "Thanks!" as she
looked to ceiling, a
Look to heaven, a look to God, with smile, God stamped
the ticket "Used!"
-- Stephen Lewis

*"Without God there is no meaning of life, for without
God, it is all random!" - Stephen Lewis*

300 and More: Soldiers of Philosophy -

History is full of miracles from the creation of man,
woman
And animals of the world, to the miracle of surviving evils
Of Satan which are born in us all, the sin of mankind
those
We cannot overcome, biggest sin lack belief in self, in
God.
Stood the ladies, children watching dead walking down
road
To the tunes of pipes, soldier warriors, weapons of state,
Truly not knowing their cause but at heart believing cause
Is just for that they have been told, Spartans of 300 King
Leonidas led into jaws of the false god, Xerxes, freedom a
Call Leonidas to Xerxes, freedom sought answer in words
of
Philosophy, Hannibal fierce, cold to core, words go a
home,
Go home rang his ears, distraught not from thousands
deaths
Of his army nor Romans, distraught knowing home is

lost, a
Soldier of the state, lover of his home, home sought answer
in words of philosophy, the king of all kings but one, the
Warrior of conquest, Alexander, soldiers of travel years of
Years fought for king knowing not why? power, wealth, of no
Answer, philosophy definitely what could it be, piece of a
Puzzle not found, in-words seeking self-love in philosophy,
Warriors of peace, soldiers too for peace can be a sword to
Many, many great warriors of peace, the one of the cross He
Greatest of all, brought meaning of life back to man, fail
Did man as did He with Adam, philosophy of it all since the
Beginning of time is found in the tears of God for failure
Of man is the failure of God, philosophy of futility answer
May God never find, His hopes, dreams may they be timeless.
-- Stephen Lewis

"The most beautiful woman in the world is the one that connects a man to God!" - Stephen Lewis

The Fall and Rise of Don Juan:

The hunt is of the stalker seeking the prey, romancing
stalker prey unclear, a
Romance has no stalker, no prey, two feeling one, respect, truth as clear as a
Love can be, all which through God's Spirit each has for other can be felt in
Their hearts, soul and mind, always being one, thinking and always needing the

Other, living in the world of God together with His
blessings, Spirit for each.
Warm touches of fingers to a lady's hand, kiss of hand,
rising eyes for stare,
Staring a flame of heat and lust into the romantic eyes of
a deer in lights of
Love of the moment, strolling down forbidden path for
emptiness of his heart a
Quest never to be filled, names and faces forgotten in the
shortest of time, a
List of faces and names created not except in memories of
'his' conquests, the
Scent of their bodies, softness of their skin, moist
refreshment of their lips
Of hunger, chase is of the women for the fox, prey chasing
the stalker, never
To be romance of the fullest, romancing his profession of
perfection, goes by
The name of those before him, Don Juan, the prince of
joy, fun, and laughter,
The prince of a black heart and self adventure of pleasure,
heartbreaker of a
Worse kind for remorse is none, smirking down road eyes
spotting for new babe
In woods, standing with ladyness near corner light in the
twilight, caught his
Eyes did she, notch another his thoughts bowing to kissed
hand, rising eyes,
His flames and lust burned from him, hers with fool gold
sparkling glittering
Sucking in her prey, Cupid's arrow found the wrong
mark, his heart, lady she a
Was, a lady of the night but for tonight she transformed a
lady of innocence,
She read her prey but not her heart, stroll of small talk,
each luring each, an

Ending until tomorrow's walk of none other, infatuation
sweated him all night
Until morrow when it arose further, words, things never
spoken before to woman,
Her coldness still but some words can melt the most
frozen hearts, night stroll
Becoming morning stroll, Don Juan discovered a love
which was waiting for her,
This night, her thoughts only of him, how could it
happen? bells, whistles, and
Fireworks all the next day, passer-by of her past swung a
piercing sword thru a
Heart Don Juan knew not he had, what a fall down rocky
cliffs of a broken love,
True love cannot be broken, climb rocky walls did he, rise
to find his love as
He chased her to the altar for the greatest of romance, he
and she felt God for
First time as they did love, His Spirit took hold of 'em, led
'em to His world.
-- Stephen Lewis

*"With strongness sometimes comes loneliness, faith in
self and God keeps strength," - Stephen Lewis*

Her Story: From Bar Stool Chair -

The strength of steel, the mightiness of diamonds, cannot
withhold the surge
From the tidal waves held within one's heart and soul,
truths of hurt, pains
Build, build and build until even God must let them go,
many keys possible an
Opening of the withholding walls, distilled drink one of
easiest key choices.
Clearing of the smoke from the clearing of the room

revealed a lonely figure
Still standing on the tallest stool, with a tallest of drinks, bartender wish
To be home, "Romance, what a crap," as she downed another sip, "Such a love,
Romance everyday, then moment for greatest romance, greatest love, pregnancy."
Beginning of a new family, the start of the most wonderful romance, that of a
Lifetime, "What a bastard he turned out to be!", tradition, ways of life only
Reason for rings of bonding, name to the baby, a hated mother, a hated father,
Hated siblings, but tradition, name, most important, birth, smiling daughter,
Brought not back the romance, the love which began it all, so was it all real
Before, fifty years, still not knew, as another sip supped gulped medicine a
Cure long sought but forgotten, now simply a hope to forget, prayers he dies
Tomorrow whenever that comes, shakes of the bartender's head he knew words of
Drunkenness are but those, sure she could not mean it, "What of your family?"
Burst of laughter so high nearly cracking glasses, know not if my answer to a
Him, tradition more so with them, name, blood oh so much, love and romance un-
Known to them, drink and bear it for that is what they did, but in all one's
Life there falls a little rain, a little relief, opened the door did a tall,
Lean lady of stylish design, a lady of class, bartender's eyes awoke wide to
See more as he approached her, thoughts abound, no

glance, slighting him did
She even as he looked back to her back, him of no
thought, no class, hugs of
Such shown emotion, kisses of such love, "Mom, let's go
to your room," smile
Of mother illuminated the dark room with a glow, with
loudness and touch of
Slurring as daughter lead her to the door, "She found
romance, I made sure,"
Bartender knew her words true, and before the door, it
opened to a tall man,
Such a gentleman shouted his appearance, assisting wife
as kissing, steady-
Ing mom, with extended arm tip of hundred dollars,
bartender smiled noticed
Love of two, romance could be no more clear, gentleman
tapped derrière his
"Kitten, I love you! wait our room we get," bartender
blushed, so did God.
-- Stephen Lewis

*"A great painter is the camera for a photo is worth a
thousand words, and it isn't temperamental," - Stephen
Lewis*

Love Need Not Conquer All: Just Two -

The war of love is unlike all other wars for the real battles
Are fought within the combatants, within each self, bias
and
Weapons from without cannot change true love for true
love is
Only created by God and His will, only God can connect
souls,
If true love fails, has God failed? Have combatants failed
to

Be conquered by God and His will, not listened to His
spirit.
"He can't love you, you senior high school, him
graduating a
PhD, you notch in belt," a wisdom from a junior, an angel
of
Trust, friend forever, bias of the world we all have, in
time
They do not exist except in our minds, the moment,
present is
Life, is love, is romance, is happiness, is all to be for God
Acts in the present, even God knows future unwritten for
sure
For He acts in the present with hope for future will be as
he
Did with creation of Man, bias of created past
unchangeable a
Moment in time only days to come may change, true love
it can
Not, God has no bias, He sees into hearts, souls, beyond
eyes
Of man can see, hear, or think, she hears all, so much
older,
You aren't bright enough, he too tall, too beauty are you,
an
Answer all had for her, her heart shouted it clear but
doubts
Of bias from those of trust, who can we trust more than
God?
She understood not language of the heart, its need by
romance
Which she sought, God tried once more with heart
murmurs of a
Systolic, diastolic, continuous kinds up and down, stop,
go a
Rhythm saying, "You love him, he you, Me both of you!",

heard
The language, the words, through the door went she, junior on
Arms of PhD with moves of moving up, tears of heart murmured,
Anger of soul propelled her to Him, then him, to get her love
From both, battle not for love conquered just two, Him three.
-- Stephen Lewis

"Understanding that which we cannot see, feel or hear, the Spirit world, is a gift of a few, only the fight between God and Satan determines good or bad," - Stephen Lewis

Cold Heart: Void World -

In the world we come bare naked, tap of butt opens eyes,
Really opened dare say not, for some see, some don't, to
See God's other world more than eyes are needed, a heart
Without heat, without coal to burn fires, a gift of soul
To the snake of spirit, the mother screamed though given
An epidural, an.another needed, doctor see could not one
Reason for the extreme pain, until form he outs swearing
Fingers pulling in, cry none he heard before, such cold,
"A heart of cold begets another heart of cold, Satan's,"
Years of raising warfare mother and child, school a come
To be, more warfare for grin, smile or laugh, coldest a
Hug maybe, years go on, good, bad, more indifference, an
evil awaited to awake his cold heart to the cold heat of
Its master, led to scent filled room of drugs, drinks, a
Void World of everything goes, awake did the child, no a
Longer a child, but opened eyes those of a child, to the
Light he could only see, above the smoke, smells, sounds
Of the evilness luring his innocence, evil doing good in

Bringing enlightenment to baby to see God's other world,
To see the Spirit of Light from Him, to receive blessing
From God to the warmth, heat of his heart's coal in its
Burning furnace creating love, want, and caring needed a
Every day, today for escaping evil, in time he grew one
To be to see the smile of his mother again, being able a
Smile back, the day came his smile awoke the heart of an.
Another escape the Void World of Satan, hell's coldness,
And enter the bathing waters of God's Spirit, His Love.
-- Stephen Lewis

*"Some things in life just seems meant to be, just so right,
especially when God is the dealer," - Stephen Lewis*

Juvenile Delinquent: Was To Be -

Fate and destiny cannot exist alone in one's soul,
They must live together to forge the paths of life
To death, coincidences uncredited actions of Lord,
God, prays are wishes, winds to God seeking divide
Guidance and judgment, decision right, left, man's.
He heard the beating of his little heart underneath
His home, piggy bank, not his, laid out with coins,
Mostly pennies and nickels, excitement lacking evil
And intent for he knew not what he did, head tapped
Dusty beam, older but as unwise, closing of closet
Door, dim light, shadowed fingers opening money bag
Fingering dollar bills, pulling two so not to be a
Discovered, static shock doorknob reward, found out
Was he, unpunished he went, bag chips under coat, a
Need he had not, caught, let go, friend not so good
He followed, eleven old high school early in hall a
Looting rooms here and there, friend got caught, he
Squeal like pig, dad, mom split before, dad mad
Heart not in beating, but did, hurt more dad, mom,
Never together again, just opposite, north of lake

Went all, juvenile nor delinquent no more? weight
On shoulders or miles from influence knew not, but
Scot-free no joy, years naive, college to come, an
Age of drugs, freedom of sex, ready is he? history
Bears not, was to be, not he, unseen fate, destiny
Of God he took, juvenile delinquent never more, a
Blessing of God but price to pay, years of years a
Torment did he, juvenile delinquent saved for what?
-- Stephen Lewis

*"Earth, Water, Fire and Air, elements of nature of God;
the nature of God is Spirit," - Stephen Lewis*

Breakout From The Corner: Jumping Life's Hurdles -

In all great monuments of the sands of the ages, in all
great
Buildings of man to withstand the winds of time, a
foundation
Of strength, fortitude, form as of Atlas, Titan, carries
them
So must children form a foundation for great societies of
men,
Women and children, themselves, sadly, mankind hasn't
learned.
In the corner of the dark room, the child played alone
with a
Doll, all content, except one watching, memories of his
child-
Hood, he played not alone, but was alone, he struggled as
his
Eyes watched the child to remember an image of his dad
and mom
From his childhood, could not, he understood the
contentment
Of the child but when asked to play, work left his mind,

child
Though not his, needed him, others did not see the building of
A foundation, he saw a hurdle in life and took a jump, played
Did he, in days and weeks he saw the child left to play alone
When not of her desire, he would play seeing her joy, growth
Of love, for those materials of building needed most a stable
Foundation for her life, work and self-needs gave way to her,
Another hurdle he took, the more she got away from the corner
Of darkness and loneliness, many could not see for they could
Not see loneliness, not feel loneliness, he understood seeing
This in his father, mother, and siblings, so many others, he
Sworn he wanted to be more, he failed so many times before, a
Thought not this time, he would jump the hurdles and not fall
To the track of the race of life, he wished he was not alone,
For the child's sake, and for his own, for doing it alone he
Had doubts, failing himself did not matter, failing her meant
He deserved to be alone, he couldn't leave her in the corner,
He asked for strength from his friend, answer he wasn't sure,
Some days he saw help coming, then other days slap downs from

His friend, he had to do it alone for no one understood, nor
Cared, a way of the world, for they couldn't see, without see-
Ing, they could not comprehend, jumping hurdle he asked once
More from his friend, "Lord, help me!", with that the chains
Once holding the child in the corner broke with the faith he
Had learned, was given, by his friend, hurdles still remain,
Hurdles will always be there, will he always be alone answer
Only his friend knows, asks only for Him to watch over her.
-- Stephen Lewis

"Sometimes silence screams out louder than actual words, just have to listen for it," - Stephen Lewis

Seen Everything: Hollow Man -

In time, everything is forgotten, even the greatest of evil,
Which will be followed by greater evils of Satan's apostles.
The doors of the smoke-filled saloon brusted open swinging a
Wide berth, tall, lean body rolled head first between tables
And chairs, final roll ended at foot of empty chair across a
Lady of fine stature, face kissing floor slowly rose rickety,
Worn chair, he sat blowing a kiss to the elegant lady, "Sir,
What's your brand," surprised, "The hardest," raise of hand,
Twist of fingers, rustle of feet, smug, pompous smile lit a

Baby face of hardness, past better times, "I've seen every-
Thing imaginable, but this, thanks!", she smiled a Mona
Lisa
Of no joke, joy he felt but the chuckle burned, bitch cross-
Ed his mind, she knew, laughing shot forth, "Here,
Abigail,"
Finger pointed to him, the names crossing his mind,
madder a
More he got, drink fueling fire, "What time is your finger-
Nail appointment," chuckling, prissy he knew a Queenie
she a
Was, drugs and more drugs, sex and more sex, sights to
make
A billy goat puke, what short life oh so much evil, tales he
Could tell her, show her, shot down throat it came, down
to
Table head flopped, conversation of images flashing mind
of
His, goose-steps, bombs, bodies, unseen gas, mass bodies
of
Bones and flesh, horrors upon horrors, "I've seen the
reels,"
"Hollow Man," he heard, awaking in a dream, maze he
stood, a
Puzzle caught his face, in time there will be light, started
He did, staggering, falling against steep walls, for blocks,
For miles, puzzled still, finger stuck in wall, with pull a
Oval odd-shaped ball stared him in the face, slick smooth
of
Wall, holes here and there, he knew, he felt the souls, the
Lives of those of the walls, Khmer Rouge, Khmer Rouge,
pains
Of torture, of lost souls, tore his mind, filled Hollow Man
With all that could be filled from wall of bones, skulls, of
Maze of Death, evil unmeasurable, evil is evil, "Awake
young

Man to the wisdom of the ages, of the universe, awake a love
You have forgotten, The Love of God," he stepped from a soft
Bed to the floor, flying young child into his arms, smell of
Tasty food, Abigail smiled glancing behind small Virgin Mary
Wooden plaque thanking Mother for answering his prayers, his
Past forgotten in mind but forever in his soul, having seen
Everything, Hollow Man no more, replacing emptiness of evil
With fillment of faith, love, goodness of woman, child, God.
-- Stephen Lewis

"When light becomes so dim, when all hope fails, true faith in God will bring back the fires of light and hope." - Stephen Lewis

Tarnishing of A Silver Spoon: A Mother's Love -

Corks popped on the news, a grandchild acoming to them,
Son had finally done good in their eyes, daughter-in-law,
Well, what can be said, the goods need to be protected by
All means, spare nothing for packaging until delivery, to
Time after, way of all other packagings to the garbage, a
Disposal of trash they thought she was, nine-months, much
Too long, expensive as hell if Joe Blow, they were not, a
Closer to Rockefeller, maybe more, oh, what show, acting
Natural to those of wealth, to those of a cold-heart, to
Those of conniving ways, hurt do not they feel, biting of
Tongues for days, weeks and months, day comes, what phony

Joy, smiles, all that goes with the game, "The glow adds
To your beauty, what happiness we will have," private it
All in the most understanding of birth rooms, the smile
The mother had, whisper by Grandma, "She is so
beautiful
Like her mother, but my child, tired you do look," back
To baby all eyes, what shall we name her, thoughts upon
Thoughts, it came, Helen Ann, the shining light of Saint
Anne, and her smile seemed such, the future so bright to
Be, in mother's arms in tightest sleep, whisper by Grand-
Pa, "She is the sweetest, my dear, you do look so tired,"
The dad weak and feeble to mom and dad, "Honey, she is
a
God-sent, I love you, you look tired and worn, just one
Thought, a trip for rest, to see the world," without a
Moment to think, a thrill of a lifetime, mother yet to
Feel, hug and smile came the excitement, Grands smile a
Beamed of working plan, mother and dad gone, Grands
will
Rule the child, only days to go, the night so rough with
Dreams of nightmares, a child calls to mother but mother
Is not the call, "Hey, you!" a heart dies sometimes never
To be reborn, sweats and the sight of the Devil in one's
Soul, soul without love of her child, a child she knew a
Not, a night of remembrance for lifetime, in the night a
Woman becomes a mother calling upon Saint Anne,
shining
Light of Mary, in the twilight of the dawn a shadow with
Bundle of sleeping joy enters the cab, "Where to Miss?"
With the words came a smile, from her heart, as well as,
God's, for He knew His plan, not the words spoken as to
The Spirit of God in the words, in the spirits of those
In the cab, they will be one for a family is in spirit
Not just blood, fight will be won with blessings of God.
-- Stephen Lewis

Writer's Dilemma: Aether of Words -

The desk born of old, ancient oak gave grandeur to the
moonlight
Which illuminated the room from the surrounding
windows, writing
Room of design for peace, thinking and creations, birth of
life,
But tonight, the doctor of words struggled and tormented
of what
To do, his elements of writing those of nature, Earth,
ground of
Human endurance, forbearance, fight for survival,
foundation all
Of which to build from, Water, emotions of highs and
lows, goods
And evils, plusses and minuses, flowing force to go forth,
Fire,
Passions, of course, of heat and light, love and romance,
animal
Lust of evolution, daring, charisma, the making of
adventure and
The spirit of force to drive the water, Air, bellowing fire
full
Blaze, stirs the winds of earth, directs water with tides of
low
And high, air forming breezes to sprout forth life's living,
the
Writer's dilemma in composing his most wonderful work
a missing,
An unknown element of nature to bring to his words,
sensation of

Lips on the hair of his neck shot sparks down spinal cord
to tip
Of his toes, fingers turning his head to hunger of her
mouth for
His, his breath taken away, dizziness never felt so good,
rising
Up with help from her arms, the tigeress devoured her
prey, lost
Of missing now found in the moonlight from above, in
the love of
His for his lover, the love of God she brought to him,
fingers a
Moment ago sleeping a deep sleep, now pounding
keyboard away and
With enthusiasm of fresh youth, for hours, maybe days,
snacks of
This and that, coffee aflowing until drained, until
exhaustion a
Final end of his writing, the moonlight he awoke with
sensations
Of lips on his neck and arms hugging his chest from
behind, "Hi,
Honey, I thought of you awhile ago, you're my
inspiration," she
Smiled for the pleasure she brought him, for the faith of
love,
His eternal love, the return of her love for God, she
smiled, a
Smile for the look of his eyes into hers, she knew she had
help-
Ed him find his answer, she felt proud of herself, she felt
love
For herself for which she had not felt since a child, the
answer
Is aether that binds elements of nature, essence of words,
gives

Substance to elements, to words, makes them what they
are, Earth
Water Fire Air, elements of nature, words, spoken Spirit
of God.
-- Stephen Lewis

*"A stage is a theatre by itself, but a theatre need not be a
stage," - Stephen Lewis*

Fighting God: Walking Away From Heaven -

He sat as a child outside the window of the church,
Words echoed through the glass, even when unopened,
With a mind innocent of the sins of the world, look
Did he to the sky for answers to his questions, God
Sent not one for all so many years listening to his
Father's preachings, with age he discovered his own
Answers without knowing Satan preys upon innocence,
Preys upon those not so innocent, the one question,
The one closest to his heart, dare not ask God for
Fear of the answer, "Why doesn't my father love me,
Why?", he knew the answer might be 'him', what did
He do not to be loved, he worked to be good, worked
To please, worked to hear "I love you!", worked to
Feel arms around him sending a spark to his heart,
Never, but to come the question, "Is there a God?",
He said "Yes," for who else could create such hate
In his soul by such ways as a forbidden love, first
Drink not to father but to God, in your eyes, more
Drinks to come, days of drugs not far behind, face
Offs with dad, not face of dad but that of God, he
Saw in the smoke, in the needles, in eyes all the
Women of empty love he gave, hurt himself and them
And the world he needed for he could not face God,
Not afraid of God but fear of the unknown losing a
Hate of a lifetime, fear of loving himself, losing

Self, a needle one more time, eyes no longer needed
But he watched it slowly ease into his veins thrill
Long lost, gates of heaven he saw, faces of Angels,
Faces of lost friends to death, faces and faces but
None touched his soul, he turned, walked away with
Tears in eyes, heard a voice say, "Son, I love you!"
He turned saw God's face, he kept walking, another
Voice he heard, did not turn, "Son, I love you, do
Forgive me, my arms await," he had forgotten how to
Smile, but he tried, he felt his heart, he felt his
Soul, he ran to his father and with a hug, looked a
Smile to Him and gave thanks, and God said, "Forgive
me, my arms await," his heart felt an embrace by God
And he awoke from seizure of the drugs, saw he Angel
Looking over him, nurse embracing his heart with her
Love of God, hazel eyes with burning green, flowing
Hair touching his cheeks, somehow he knew all would
Be good, he would be good, both would be good, toget-
Her they would be good, she told him with her first
Touch of her love for him from God, he heard words a
Blazing through the glass, innocence was his, again.
-- Stephen Lewis

*"In doing my best, I have not created any right or
wrong," - Stephen Lewis*

Fallen Soldiers: Faith of Honor -

The old lady had eyes of the ages, winkles above and
below, tautness
Of skin and frail body, loud explosions boomed around
her, which war
Does not matter, futility of war is the fact they never end,
yell of
Charge into flashes of gunfire and roars of cannons and
grapeshot, a

March of flesh, blood and bones, to be torn, ripped, from
human form
To deformity, living horror for many lost souls, living,
breathing a
Life question, "I wish I would have died," the heat from
the burning
Boilers of the warship's fire room gave men feelings of a
sun's heat
They were sure, if not for burning torture, fear of a shell
piercing
Wooden desk would eat courage from their plates, a day
the sound was
Heard, "Oh, my God," valley below, the Celts lined forest
edge sight
Of the Romans above, screams which would frightened
the dead echoed
Up the Land of Gaul, certain death awaited them as
Caesar smiled his
Famous smile of question, "Et tu, Brute?" knowing
Brutus had signed
His faith, Caesar's and Brutus' as well, before time of
settlers and
Soldiers from the East, in the early morning rays,
Mohawk warriors a
Most feared of tribes, raided sleeping village of unaware
victims of
Peaceful tribe, conquest fights not fair, victors live on to
fight a
Future day, war with the Mohicans to come with, in
Algonquin tongue,
Mohawk conveys flesh-eating, cannibal feasting, what a
sight, "Civil
Exists not in war," last explosions rocked foundation of
old lady's
Shelter, ceiling flaked dust down upon her head, "Citizens
do not ex-

Ist in War! We are all soldiers," whistling she heard and
shook head
As her doomsday crushed down upon her, all fallen
'soldiers' of war
Die in faith of honor, God blesses and treats them so, at
the gates
Of Heaven, she found youth with softness of skin, firm
body and eyes
Looking upon her lost love, his youth, strength, a love for
eternity.
-- Stephen Lewis

*"Freewill, a blessing or curse, we all must decide for
ourselves," - Stephen Lewis*

Street Urchin: A little rat -

Scene could take a heart away, small child under warm
quilt
Near soft, lit fireplace, cookies on nightstand, warm milk,
Grandma nestled near her side, "Grandma, tell me the
story
Again, please," Grandma knew the story well, she had
lived
It, for her child, she would tell it over and over, "It all
Started on a cold night,"... a new recruit returned home
by
The darkened alley after an eye-opening day to harshness
of
Being police officer, fatigue enlightened his nerves to the
Slightest sound, a rustling sound to his rear, black image
He caught but not sure what, then to the front, the
sounds
Again with more image, what was it, finally home, no
sound
Sleep, another day, another night, more sounds and

images,
More restless sleep, weeks go by and stories he hears from
Those fellow officers of the street urchin roaming nights,
Harm to none, uncountable thefts, for years and years, and
Only blurry images here, there, everywhere, he thought how
Do I catch thee, little cheese for a little rat, break for
The day, quick alley visit setting trap, anxiety for night
To anticipate, to anticipate his catch, would it work, yes
For sure as stepping to alley, dead stop first sound, none
Move second sound, no movement, third sound closer still,
One more sound oh so close, click remote, lights flash up
Blinded staring eyes, little rat by the lights, officer by
Beauty of such not a little rat, dirt, filth, ripped wear
Covering unlawful showing, quick lunge of hand to arm, she
Struggled with such strength, from hand to hands, wrapped
Arms, as her head swirled crazily with wild abandon, stop
As stone her face as eyes caught his, their first sight of
God together, hours of talk on street side curb, stories a
Writer could not word, hers of years on streets, in alleys
Of home, his of years seeking a home within, until now, he
Nor she understood until streetlight went out, above a Old
Jackson, rearing horse, risen hat, sat star shining bright
With a smile in a lonely sky... Grandma looked at child and
Closed eyelids... "and God said to us, live a long, happy,
And joyful life, and our new lives begun," kissing forehead
A hand appeared over her shoulder, holding hand she

rose to
His arms, heavenly embrace and a kiss forever more to
Amen.
-- Stephen Lewis

*"The greatest riches in the world are the children for
they can see the 'real' world; most adults forget what
they knew as children, they grow up, the shame," --
Stephen Lewis*

The Night of Hale: The Tree Awaits -

He was hung with an unmarked grave, legends have it,
The soul of a spy cannot rest with a grave unmarked.
Greenhouse doors closed with force by guards, Nathan
Had no thought of tomorrow, only missing holy bible,
Maybe a clergyman, sure not, aware now aroma smells,
Eyes focusing on reddish of flowers, beauty her lips
Same color, over there flowers of pink, shade cheeks
She had, search of the greens found closest one eyes
Of hazel, that night of finding love in her words in
Deepness of her eyes, hands of strength seeking soft
Heart of understanding, romance she never felt once,
He willing to be her one, night ending but not love,
Notes, letters of words, hollow words filled spirit,
Filled romance of love, promises of future to ever-
More, thanking prayers to God for treasures found in
Each other, suddenly a new smell of a sulking flower
Brought the horror of reality back to him, a British
Round ball shot in fear in crowd, down she fell, all
Crashed in his life, what is it now to lose his life
From a tree, in the flowers and plants find he faith
From God in returning her to him for one night, open
Did the doors to the awaiting tree, larynx itched in
Touch of rope, feet swung in twitches until death of
Breath, spirit in abode of lost souls never to see a

Heaven or hell, the shovel tossed the last dirt out,
In went Hale's body with spirit of soul, silent came
The night as did his love with smelly sulking flower
Of repent to mark his grave, together to heaven they
Went to be embraced by blessings God and His Angels.
-- Stephen Lewis

*"The greatest land of discovery is the mirror!" - Stephen
Lewis*

Candlelight In The Sun:

Swords, Wands, Pentacles and with a flip, Cups, Queens
of the Tarots,
The eyes of Madame Marie, native of the Tarot language,
reader of the
Cards of life, "My son, in the future you shall meet the
One, a queen
To lead you out of the darkness, to lead you into the light,
a queen
Of all Queens, past, present, future, and heaven she rules,
rules all
In her kingdom with wisdom, compassion,
understanding, yet, lonely is
She for one to rule her, are you the one?" with the
greatest strength
He could find he held his laughter, calmly said, "How
much will it be
To be the one?", without emotion and sternest of faces,
"The price is
Yours to decide to pay for it will not be coins," as her head
lowered
Into the smoke of the incense, "No more!", "When do I
pay?", answered
Not for an eternity as he turned to leave, murmured as a
sigh, "Pray

I will for you," head turning back to see her figure leave into back
Of tent, carnival lights, sounds, liveliness abound took away mystery
Of her words, soon forgotten words they became, the night joy and fun
Seemed neverending, all rides, games, more he saw until one in corner
Distance field, dim lit sign, "Queen of the Mystic Bayou" seer of all
Fate and destiny read the second line, line none, push of a tent flap
And he entered with odd, eery feelings including call of curiosity of
The unknown, "Two tickets, please," he heard, holding out two, wisped
Away in the darkness as entrance appeared to amazement of his eyes, a
Room of such size his mind whizzed to know illusion must it be, table
Of round, yet not round he sat, light of single crystal candle holder
Ablazed the colors shooting from the crystal around the tent, a sight
Not to be believed, turning, twisting head, dizzy near, enter figure
Of royal purple cowl hood, sat did the figure, long tanned soft hands
Slowly lowered the hood revealing closed eyes, blackish hair of curls
For envy, lips of the Nile painted red, all sounds stopped except his
Heartbeat at the opening of her eyes, greenish with tints of blue, an
Inferno flame of coldness shot into his soul, perfection but for lack

Of a smile, her arms reached to the center of oval disk around candle
Stick spreading open her hands, somehow knowing he reached his hands
Into hers, breath left his body as did his strength, firmly stood did
He somehow raising with her, her name appeared in his thoughts as did
Her story, in wonder, he knew his name, his story unfurled, unraveled
To her, in a half blink the coldness of her eyes bursted and inflamed
Into passion, conviction, desire and need, in a new breath, so did he
With a love for her, yet more, a love from a seed to a love of a tree
Bearing His gifts of faith and belief in him, all doubts, all wonders
Of if, were gone, he knew he was loved by Him, His spiritual daughter
As well, why he asked not, question not the Lord of all would he, ask
Not the past but accept the future, "Are you the one," he heard words
Said, "to be by my side for eternity," Madame Marie he saw in images,
Remembered the price would not be coins, he chuckled, "The price?", a
Reply, "Your soul!", the future he saw at that moment, to be one with
Her for all times, an endless romance created by God, "For sure," his
Lips said, his soul became one with hers for the greatest romance one
Can be gifted by God, as if from awakening from deep sleep, the tent

Was no more, where they stood he did not know, but candlelight filled
The heavens as the sun radiated down with God's smile, hands together
And closeness as could be, they kissed as their eyes met, when closed
By passion and desire, their eyes opened to a new world, life as one.
-- Stephen Lewis

"The shortest distance between two points is a straight-line; in life, a straight-line is not as colorful." - Stephen Lewis

Richard Richard: What's In A Name-

Through the doorway he quickly entered to behind podium,
Nerves showed, sweat in cold room, most eyes staring his
Every move so to read new professor, book pulled from an
Old style briefcase sparkling with newness, next chalk a
Teaching commodity of the time, attendance he dread pull-
Ing sheet next, chalk to the board, course rubric, then a
Title of course, of course name next, what laughter when
Pronouncing his name, Richard Richard, which came first a
Thought they all had, knew he focus of their jovial burst
Unstoppable from day of birth naming by mother, Richard,
From Dad, Richard, oh, what a hatred had he for his name,
First day teaching, in front numerous faces, how could he
Prepare for his name, then to say his name in reverse mis-

Take we all make with last name being first, Richard, next
Richard, how embarrassment red cheek, further red
when did
He try to fix, from book he read word for word whole
class
Time with sweat of red down his face, nerves on nerves,
he
Wished with time, hands held face down on desk
repeating a
Name which he knew not first or last, Richard, a voice he
Heard say, thanks for the joy Richard Ree-shard, or is it
Ree-shard Richard, name means not what I see in your
soul.
-- Stephen Lewis

*"The body doesn't make the person, the person makes
the body; beauty isn't with the body, beauty is with the
person." - Stephen Lewis*

The Hindenburg Beginning?

Sieg Heil! sounded in the air shouted by feverish,
bloodthirsty,
Everyday people driven by an oratorical madman, his
driven evils
Blinding all but a few, even those to be future victims of
purge
Of the unfit, ethic cleansing, the final solution, shouting
top
Of their lungs for pride of Germany, mighty Hindenburg
dirigible
Largest airship the world ever seen floated into the gray
clouds
Covering the land and the world, looking down a
promenade window
To the chorus of hate below elderly man's tears fell upon

glass,
Soon his eyes lost sight through the smeared glass, cloudy
eyes,
Never to see his homeland again, life-long dreams never
to have
An ending he surely knew for land of the free a new
beginning to
What he knew not for one of his age, fainting back into
Writing
And Reading Room rounded by Otto Arpke's paintings
world scenes,
Falling into his chair of his new writing, "The Beginning",
his
Dreams written for new land for one of years to go, just
dreams,
Wishes to God, his own, the drink went down his throat
smoothly
To wash away his sorrows, the tall, younger lady sat near,
book
Opening to a page, for such beauty lines of dread, pains,
fears,
Could be seen along her red lips, below her hazel eyes,
blonde
Hair brushed to cover unseen, inner horrors she lived,
sought to
Escape, face into book, scarf used for sniffles, soon
forgotten
Were his fate and destiny, standing tall as could be, proud
as a
Peacock he walked to her side, even with such sadness,
such lost
Of humanity, her sniffles brought unknown joy to same
sadness of
His, same lost of humanity, joy in such a world now and
to come,
Priceless he knew, "May I sit?" shot from his voice, a

something
New to him, outgoing not, for her, answer not to come for action
He took and sat, head turning, her eyes meeting his, she knew to
Such joy she would embrace if not past horrors, stand tall must
She, but such love she felt never before, yet such horrors close
All doors, she saw not his age but his compassion, his sorrows,
His longings for what she sought, weakness she dare not show for
Horrors close all doors, could he open them? he prayed to God to
Award him the key to those doors and what laid beyond, if only
He knew, God ordained them meet, swinging open those doors, the
Doors of one, theirs, words but more than words spoken and felt
Between two fighting to become one, hours, days unrecorded time,
Dreams, wishes, hopes of two now those of one, age and horrors
Broken barriers by love, happiness and joy, strengthened by God,
Stewards sternly announced the coming landing, hand squeezed an-
Other hand, smile to smile, heart to heart, they walked to the
Promenade in the light of God, and in the blaze of fire to come,
Through God's grace cleansed from the past living and horrors to
Live future years of God's blessings through coming

catastrophes.
-- Stephen Lewis

*"Wealth is power, power is not always wealth." -
Stephen Lewis*

The Magic of Joy: God's Secret or Witchcraft?

The cold water of hell ran against the skin of the giggling
baby,
He being held by mother into the river of Styx entering
his world
With joy from the witchcraft of the times, or God's secret
untold
To the world, joy of living, joy of becoming greatest
warrior of
All times, joy of finally finding love of the ages the last
days
Of Troy only to lose joy to pain of the piercing arrow,
magic of
The true meaning of Joy unfound by all, even Achilles,
fluffiness
Of Love and Happiness blinds all to God's Secret or to
witchcraft
To those nonbelievers, magic of Joy found by so few, gift
of God,
Or spell of witchcraft, only with such is it possible to
discover
That secret, the secret to make love, happiness the words
people
Believe they are, for without Joy they are not, the ground
felt a
Coldness of Death as the cabin of driver came down upon
him, hand
And arm powerless to onslaught of weight, breathless
then death a

Blessing from suffering, imagine did the child in his mind was he
To blame, what did he miss, new to the lost of life of another, a
Freezing moment of life to take a life, life goes on with a quest
By child, what is the meaning of it all, fault of wreck was mine?
To find Holy Grail one must know what they seek, blindly reaching
Out most of his life for love, happiness, discovers hollowness of
Them without solid filling of Joy, the Joy he found in her filled
His emptiness of love and lack of happiness, her eyes, her smile,
Poured into his hollow heart, filled happiness into his soul, but
The Magic of Joy, it's secret, is of God, for in God there's Joy.
-- Stephen Lewis

"Remember yesteryears, live the present, await the future," - Stephen Lewis

? More:

Time stopped to be awoken in slow dull flash of light,
Ceiling tiles filled the sky of his newly opened eyes,
Muffled sounds echoed stirless air of sterilized smell,
Geared wheels of his stunned mind moved with a thought,
Words, stories mattered not for three days lost of life
To mystery of God's winds which blew from that night on
Seemed neverending, filled with dreams, wishes, night-
Mares some from God, some from once angel, named

Satan,
Which were which, he could not tell, only let God lead,
Lead him to His promised land, happiness, boundless and
Tastiest of fruits, Moses be he not, questions of faith
Wielded by Satan tempted to satisfy thirst of happiness
And days forgotten loneliness, fall he not as prey to a
Hungry Satan, spit into those fiery eyes did he, price
Will he pay continued search to satisfy his thirst of a
Life of ordinary man, a wife of God to live by his side
As his equal in both love and life, he awaits decision
Of God, his faith weakened by Satan, an asked question
Of God's winds from years ago, "? More," will God give
The answer after all these years, or journey continued.
-- Stephen Lewis

"There are no tough days except when you don't have friends," - Stephen Lewis

Creation of Man: Sonnet Four of ?

A thought, first beginning, alone no more,
Mind, think, imagine, brain, head his most core,
Land dust with water He shapes to adore,
Arms, legs, lean neck and body, hands, feet allure,
Flawless for sure, yet, God's last gift did tore,
Perfection no more, freewill bloody gore,
Meaning, purpose unknown gifts to be lore,
Quest begins not alone woman to fore,
Travel or race side-by-side to yore,
Life not endless so he speeds to a score,
Not of flesh, of heaven, God's open pore,
Obstacles abound drilling he would bore,
With grace accepted God's dessert s'more,
Happiness, love, sandwiched by two, she's zore.
-- Stephen Lewis

*"The key to yoga, or any exercise, is proper breathing," -
Stephen Lewis*

Mystery of Faith: Sonnet Three of ?

God goes by many names, one said Mr. Kait.
Child cries for know not why coming of fate,
Life such joy, just thinking Lord being zate,
Cometh day waking finding living vate,
Many more days come in state of wate,
Unseen His ways but belief He's nait,
How after so many years filled up hate?
Ceremonially seeking his Cait,
Here, there until Godsent her of un-jait,
Her eyes looked away, he entered a fait,
Understand not though everyone said bate,
God stood by his side giving him faith's sate,
With God's eyes she saw she more than a sait,
Love, romance theirs God's faith made him pate.
-- Stephen Lewis

*"Reason why many people may not understand you,
they don't care to," - Stephen Lewis*

Roses Serenade: Sonnet Two of ?

Gilded wrought iron rails flowing roses,
Designs of two's love and romance poses,
Voice of an Angel, sweet words of proses
Sung below about those figures loses
His heart to her with each word in the winds,
From above her soul melts them in all binds
Imaginable by God and all minds,
The white rose blushes with love's truth it pines
For the caring of the yellow rose finds
Rose of pale pink seeking happiness dines

On passion orange bouquet roses wines
Lilac mystic enchantment rose, it vines
A rainbow color roses of all kinds
But Crimson Rose true lovers' to the nines.
-- Stephen Lewis

*"Sometimes, one has to break their mold to find
happiness," - Stephen Lewis*

Jubilee - Sonnet One of ?

The moment brought enslavement to the teat,
Curdling of the nipple's milk due to hot heat,
Refusal of slave to admit de-feat,
Years of years misery, darkened blue deep,
Journey continued inch by day to feet,
More than Love sought by God's grace not to weep,
Fall one day, rise another peep,
Pulling life's rope climbing hill only peat,
How, why explain not the Angel took beet,
Voice shouted sweetness to the heart of beep,
Soar into the light with the hope of beat,
The silver bell rings end of round take seat,
Ring again silver bell God said neat,
Jubilee! Slave no more but to love keep.
-- Stephen Lewis

*"Finding Heaven doesn't mean you have found
Happiness," - Stephen Lewis*

Sonnet to Elizabeth

Your words ring in my ears towards my heart,
As I read your sonnets my love grows more,
More for the one I love for evermore,
Cannot count the ways I love her for her,

God sayth, wait not for heaven, love today,
Say to love for love sake, I say not, for
My sake I love her, sake of our one soul,
Sake of love's eternity, end of time,
Beloved, my Beloved, I think not
Of those days to come, heaven earth all one,
Dull Atheists love of one through God unknown,
Elizabeth, thou words hold back feelings,
Tears, crying of the heart, fear not my love,
For my true love is for another one.
-- Stephen Lewis

"Sometimes, gotta go thru ALL HELL for Him to find you." -- Stephen Lewis

To Know The Winds:

In the beginning, God *summoned* the winds to create the
Earth,
The winds the tips of his fingers molding earth, dust to
man,
The eagle looked down to the lands below floating on the
gust
Of winds, true freedom ever to be known, soaring alone
in air
Knowing the winds govern the world by the will, grace of
God,
The eagle smiled for he understood the winds and the
sailing
Through life, he learned not to fight the winds, life gusts a
Challenge of flight, a challenge from God to strengthen
eagle
To the ways of evil, without the strength of God eagle
knew a
Life of fulfillment, happiness impossible, a life serving
Him

With the winds to be unknown, without the winds one falls and
Falls into the pits of fire, into the temptations and sins of
The other, of Satan, a prince in his own mind for though once
An angel, no more, evil knows no prince or God, evil is evil,
Satan is pure evil and immortal only through souls of others,
The winds of God keeps the eagle from the evils of Satan and
Eternal damnation, by following winds the eagle follows God's
Will, shadows of the wings of the eagle fell upon the man and
He took flight into the winds of God with a silver shield and
Golden sword, his falling into pits of fire no longer, rising
Instead towards the Sun, towards true meaning of finding love
Of God, towards the Son holding His hand battling evils, more
Evils one cannot imagine, all falling to His golden sword the
War never-ending until knowing the winds, entering the gates
Of Heaven with the eagle, the love of God, to know the Winds.
-- Stephen Lewis

"People do make me laugh. People say they believe in God, but they don't hear HIM Talk. People talk TO GOD, People don't talk WITH GOD. God "loves" conversation! He just shakes His head." - Stephen Lewis

"The good things about photos and videos are the memories; the 'worst' thing about photos and videos are the memories," — Stephen Lewis

"Without inspiration, one shouldn't write," – Stephen Lewis

"God governs ALL storms, including ones of love." -- Stephen Lewis

"How does one give up on some'thing' one Truly Loves!" -- Stephen Lewis

EXTRA: Some Old Writings

Jean--The Garden

When I told "Jean" I loved her,
She laughed and laughed.
As I walked away in a daze,
Laughter rang loudly in my ears.
I awoken from my depressed trance,
Only to find myself in a garden.

Pale blue skies bring to mind
  Her crystal, diamond blue eyes,
Her cherry red lips,
  Are captured in the blood red roses,
The cold, white marble of the motionless statue
  Resembles the snow whiteness of her skin.
The loving softness of her body
  Embodies the gentle, green grass,
The sparkling, fresh water of the fountain flows
  With the carefreeness of her abundant, brownish hair,
The singing of the minstrel sparrows
  Only mock the sweetness of her tender voice,

The crisp, clean, country air
    Makes for longing of her warm embrace.

My heart is broken,
But not forever,
For life goes on,

Until my love
For Jean subsides,
The "Garden"
Shall comfort me.
– Stephen Lewis

My Poetry

The words may not all rhyme,
The lines may be miss 'stood
And outside the guides of poetry law.
Yet hidden meaning one must search,
To cherish the value of my poetry.
– Stephen Lewis

Nelleen

Red, yellow, golden leafs of Lady Autumn,
Covers the ground as far as eye could see.

Sounds of approaching footsteps did I hear,
On the moist, morning leaves,
Of the clear, clean, noiseless woods.

As footsteps got nearer and nearer,
Behold! A wonder of the world.
Venus and Helen to shame,

For she is lovelier than a moonfull night.

As distance drew near, I did fear.
Scared, not I,
But temptation to hard to bear,
Neither Hun of Rome
Nor Nazi of Louvre was I,
And neither did I want to be,
But with embrace,
Rome and Louvre mind forgot.

When sun arose, I awoke with pleasures,
Joys, and memories of night before.
Memories of sweet fragrances and warm touches,
But where is Nelleen.

Laugh leaves and trees of Jolly,
For thou knows where she has gone,
Yet, thou cannot tell me.

Nelleen was thee fancy of mind,
Or was thee real warmth and form.
Truly it does matter,
For I love thee.
– Stephen Lewis

The Dying of the Flame

The flame from the burning cross shone upon the earth,
As the flame flicked light rays, faces of men could be seen.
Good men had faces of sorrow for they feared evil.
Faces of joy had evil men for evil loves evil.
With "the dying of the flame", God looked away.
Men then contemplated the self-inflicted evil.
Yet, it was too late to save their eternal souls.

– Stephen Lewis

Marty

Her name is Marty,
Who is quite naughty.
Wiggles her hips
And smacks her lips,
To see young men,
Older than ten,
Wish, hope, and pray,
It is all for pay.
– Stephen Lewis

Valentine Love

The warmth from your Venus body,
Melts my cold, cold heart.
The sweetness from your Angel voice,
Brings joy and love to my dark soul.
The gleam from your piercing eyes,
Unlocks the door to my longing passions-
The passion of wanting to love you.

But it is my love of you
Which keeps me from your arms,
For it would be unforgivable, ungodly,
To ravage such innocence, such purity.

However, it is that time of year again,
Valentine Day- the day reserved for lovers.
Now I shall know
If you love me as I love you,
For I shall send to you a card,

Expressing the love I have for you
As a woman-- a thing of beauty and love,
And as a person- equal in creation and thought.
– Stephen Lewis

Dead Man's Eyes

What lovely crowd I do see.
Nephews, nieces, cousins by the scores.
Sons and daughters are first in line.
Dear wife where are you?
Behind the procession I see you.
It is fitting you are last in line,
For of all you hate me most.
Marrying a dead man you thought.
Too bad I lived twenty years too long,
For now your young beauty is far gone.
And to make matters even worst,
I left you not a blessed dime.
My fortunes shall go to charity.
Curse me sons, daughters, and wife,
But I could not leave my money to spendthrift hands.
God, I am yours to do with as you please.
Heaven or hell, I do not care.
Just to see the mourning of my false love ones,
Has made my eternity worthwhile no matter where I go.
– Stephen Lewis

Valentine Day

I give to you this day,
The love I bear in my heart.
But much more do you deserve,
For you, woman, are my strength.

Walk not in front of me,
Walk not on side of me,
But walk behind me.

Not 'cause you are unequal
In creation or thought,
But to catch me before I fall.

It is with your support,
That I, mere man, survives.
It is your softness and warmth,
That comforts and strengthens me
To meet the toils and agonies
Of the cruel and harsh world.

Possession of your love,
Is the only treasure I seek.
It is why that today,
I shower you with my love.

But I shall on this day,
Also show to you,
The appreciation I truly have for you.

To know someone loves you,
Is the greatest gift of all.

But appreciation must he also have,
For how else shall you know,
That he faithfully loves you.

Today is Valentine Day,
The day of roses and wine,
And I must say,
I love and appreciate you.

So should I forget this year,
To repeat these soon forgotten
But not lost words,
Look back to today, Valentine Day,
And know I do love and appreciate you.

May I be blessed on Valentine Day
With your love and appreciation.
– Stephen Lewis

Imagination

Imagination, run free and wild.
Oranges circle overhead,
The swirling reds
And the streaking blues.
Spots of yellow and green
Flash on and off.
Triangles and squares
Of black and white
Do not fade at all.
Colors and movement never cease,
And all I did was...
Close my eyes and 'imagined'.
– Stephen Lewis

When

When her angel blue eyes--
    Like blue of a clear, summer day--
        Look at me,
I feel she can see my inner soul.

When her sweet, pleasant voice--
    Like singing birds of a cheerful morning--
        Rings out,
I eagerly grasp each syllable, consonant, and vowel.

When her gentle, soft hands--
    Like white velvet of a queen's robe--
        Are near,
I refrain from reaching out and caressing them.

When she gracefully wets--
    Like dew wets an early morning rose--
        Her ruby red lips,
I dream of the day I may kiss them.

When her warm, pulsating body--
    Like warmth of a campfire on a cool night--
        Is approaching,
I most profoundly want to hold her near to me.

When she carelessly wiggles--
    Like a ship on ocean waves--
        Her round hips,
I think of the endless pleasures I may one day enjoy.

When--only the "Fates" shall know.
– Stephen Lewis

Her Radiant Smile

But add to the beauty of--
  Hazel green eyes, ruby red lips, lovely white nose.
All who bathes in the life giving rays of--
  Rejoice in their new found feelings of pleasure and joy.
All women are envy of--

Even Venus, goddess of love.
Evil men dare not glance at--
  For fear their evil souls will turn to gold.
Good men seek to look at--
  For enlightenment of their discontented souls.
I journey for a change to see--
  Because of the warmth it brings to my deep soul that is
  cold.
Oh! What a God blessing is--
For all, including myself, love-- "Her Radiant Smile".
– Stephen Lewis

I sign all my writings because I still can't believe it is me
writing a book. I hope this isn't my last book, but I lost
my inspiration to write, so unless I re:discover it or
another inspiration, it mostly like will be my last writing,
my last book. God, Bless!